Thumbelina:
The Bride Experiment

Sky Sommers

Published by Sommersby OÜ

Sommers
by

Illustrations by MadMadam and Lottabel.
Cover art by Rusham Riyas
Editor S. Nanda

ISBN: 9789949881703

Printed and bound in Estonia
by AS Pakett, Laki 17, Tallinn, Estonia
pakett@pakett.ee

Other books by Sky:
Goddesses: Hubble, Bubble, Toil and Trouble
Someone To Watch Over Me
King of Time

For Mun Mun,
for promising to bite at the ankles of anyone who
will even think of hurting her friends.

She can, too.
She's the right pixie height.

ACKNOWLEDGEMENTS

This book wouldn't be here without my editor, who worked at it through constant back pain and nagging author self-doubt Whatsapp messages. She always asks just the right thing – even if it turns out I need to completely rewrite the pessimistic ending. Any remaining mistakes and typos are my own and inserted as a manic final final final rewrite post-edit.

Many thanks to my illustrators, Emmi and Lotabel, for awesome fairy and critter drawings - the story wouldn't be the same without them.

Table of Contents

Prologue

With an hour to go until midnight Morgana stood outside the twin tulip doors and let the crickets usher her in.

The key in ensnaring the prince was arriving fashionably late.

That and glamour.

An entire roomful of fairies hushed when she entered.

Glamour she could do.

Fluttering her iridescent wings, Morgana floated up to the royal couple. In flight she noticed the intricate Celtic detail of the queen's crown. By the time she curtsied, a bracelet of a similar design had formed on her wrist.

'Welcome! Welcome!' the Fairy Queen took her hand and squeezed it gently. 'What is your name, princess? I do believe you are not from these parts?' the queen gushed.

Assumptions were always good.

'Morgana, Your Majesty,' she curtsied to both monarchs and added 'from...Camelot.'

'Welcome, Princess Morgana of Camelot!' the king announced to the room.

Morgana lowered her eyes.

Not quite, but assumptions were always good.

The music started up again. So did the whispers.

The Fairy Queen nudged her son, 'Theodore, perhaps the princess wishes to dance...'

The prince awoke from his naked admiration of the newcomer and said 'May I have this dance, Princess Morgana?'

Morgana smiled and let herself be led to the dance floor. *En route* she picked up details of the design of one fairy's dress sleeve, another's delicate amethyst ring, the translucent golden bow of the third one's shoe, and added to her outfit on the go.

She had always been good at jaw-dropping first impressions. Second impressions just solidified the initial awe.

Even when turning from a bloodthirsty harpy into the Lady of the Lake, she had transfigured in style. Now that the new King of Camelot had pulled the sword from the stone she had been guarding and she was left jobless[1], it was time to find her a kingdom where they had a need for a fairy queen.

Except the position was already taken.

For now.

Marrying an heir to the throne was probably better for the morale of her future subjects than taking the kingdom by force.

She had contemplated that as well, of course.

From human height, all the flower-colonies she had seen on her arrival had emulated the zillion shades of all the colours of the rainbow, each colony their own hue and their own species of flower. There were Caribbean blue daffodils and orange callas, pink daisies and fiery tulips, peach forget-me-nots and lilies of the valley so purple they seemed positively black.

She had caused quite the panic, towering in her original form over a sea of flowers. Then and there, Morgana had decided that she'd rather rule over the happy sort of fairies. She could do without the high-pitched screams and weeping.

Morgana had promptly chosen a colony of tulips and morphed into a miniature version of herself. Plus the wings.

With the imminent threat gone, the fairies had quickly returned back to normal.

Even their Spring Ball had gone ahead, same as every year.

And now, here she was.

Dancing with her future husband, if she had her way.

By the looks Prince Theodore was casting, her future was looking exactly as she had planned.

Fancy that. You CAN plan true love.

Now a disappearing act at midnight, followed by being happily reunited with an heir to the throne and voila!

Phase one of her conquest would be complete.

She'd be the wife of a fairy prince.

Which means she could be a Fairy Queen someday.
Someday soon.
How long did fairies live, anyway?

1. How long did fairies live, anyway?

Chapter 1. The Harvesting

'We have another one for you, Your Majesty,' said a cockchafer, landing on the window-sill.

'Did you goad another fairy about her looks so she took her life, the husband followed shortly and now we have another orphan?' Morgana asked without a hint of humour.

'We got two birds with one stone,' the May bug said and wriggled its feelers. 'And possibly more.'

'Explain!' Morgana demanded.

'It was Lorelei,' the bug said smugly.

'Lorelei? My sister-in-law Princess Lorelei? You dared to harvest from the royal household?'

The bug bowed.

'What good would my niece be to me in this endeavour even if she and her parents are no longer in line for the throne?' Morgana spat.

Not only had the bugs done her a disservice in terms of a useless candidate that would not procure a bloodline, they had dispatched her only confidante who always understood, who always took her side and who, of course, knew nothing of her secret plans.

The cockchafer fidgeted about, trying to find a better perch. 'What do you care how and where you get the orphans from, as long as you get them?' it asked.

'Careful! Or I'll have to discontinue the shipments of leaves and flowers to your trading house and I don't think your queen would like that,' Morgana said.

'Careful with the threats, Your Majesty or we won't goad another vain fairy this month and then you'll have to wait a year before you get to harvest another orphan. You wanted twelve, right? Still two to go, I believe...?' the bug wriggled its feelers.

Something fell and shattered to pieces behind Morgana.

'I see Prince Edwin is finding his feet,' the bug said and peeked into the innards of the room.

Morgana eyed her toddler thoughtfully and smiled, 'Yes, they grow up so fast...'

Which was why she did want two more orphaned fairy girls this year and this left her with only three more weeks to procure them. Only then would she be good and ready for phase four of her plan.

Out loud she said, 'Why you May bugs only allow yourself to frolic for five to seven weeks a year, I have no clue, you live to be a hundred!'

'We do everything in moderation, Your Majesty,' the cockchafer said. 'That and frolicking for only five to seven weeks a year is how we live to be a hundred.'

'Except when it comes to goading vain fairies,' Morgana scoffed. 'Then you forget about moderation.'

'Goading maybe ten fairies out of whom five are vain enough to believe they actually are ugly - all in the space of five to seven weeks as you said...that IS moderation. Be grateful that we're asleep for the rest of the year. Otherwise you'd have to start building orphanages housing hundreds,' the bug said and buzzed off.

2. *'Row, row, row your boat.'*

Chapter 2. A Perfect Day

Etta yawned and stretched, kicked off her rose petal covers and only then opened her eyes.

Another beautiful day.

Etta climbed out of her bed and felt the walnut under her feet.

Wobbles easily.

The old woman hadn't poured the water into the plate yet.

'Good morning, Etta!' a booming voice said as a huge face approached Etta's walnut.

'Morning, mother!' Etta said and smiled up at the woman towering over her.

'Slept in your clothes again, did you?' The woman tsk-tsk-ed as Etta shrugged. 'Do you want to explore the house today or row on the lake?' the woman whispered.

Etta peeked outside. Exploring the garden would be nice, but she knew that that was not going to happen. Not since she got too curious about why the woman kept so many sheds out back. She had been confined to indoor fun for months now. Etta sighed, 'I climbed the kitchen cabinets yesterday, maybe some water sports would be good today?' she said and the woman nodded.

'Warm or cold?' she asked.

'Luke-warm, if you please,' Etta yelled after the woman who was already shuffling away.

Minutes later, she was back and Etta grabbed the walls of her walnut as it started rocking gently.

Etta watched the artificial waterfall from the tea cup fill the plate around her home.

When the rocking stopped and the plate was full, Etta stretched and dove in.

She resurfaced smiling, 'How lovely, just the perfect temperature, thank you, mother!'

The woman smiled, 'You're welcome, dear. We both know I'm not your mother, but I still like it when you call me that,' she said. 'I'm just blessed the witch magicked you for me from a flower.'

Yeees. And their conversation about how girls springing from flowers factored into genetics had been postponed time and again, Etta thought.

As Etta splashed about, she asked, 'Uh, do you...ufff...have a new boat...uff...for me today?'

There had to be a reason why the woman had luke-warm water on standby.

'Oh, you clever girl, you've spoilt the surprise again!' the woman admonished.

'What colour is it?' Etta asked.

From behind her, the woman produced a boat, which consisted of two tulip leafs sewn together.

The boat was bright red.

'Ooh, my favourite colour!' Etta squealed, treading water and caught a mouthful.

'There, there, cough it out!' The woman put her hand into the water so Etta could stand up and set the tulip gently onto the surface.

Etta let herself be helped out of the water and into the boat.

As soon as she was settled, the woman produced a tooth-pick for an oar. 'There!'

'Row, row, row your boat,' Etta started singing as the woman had taught her.

The woman sat by the table and watched her frolic.

'What shall we talk about today, mother?' Etta asked.

'I thought, maybe you might be interested in quantum physics,' the woman asked.

'What is that? Oh, do tell?' Etta said. 'You know how I love to learn new things. I particularly loved the survival camp exercise we did that day in the garden,' Etta added.

The woman shook her head, 'You know that it's because of your health, dear...' she said.

'But I'm feeling great and I'm not ill...' Etta started.

The woman kept shaking her head.

'What if I put on ALL of my dresses, I'd be warm then...' Etta suggested.

'No,' the woman said.

'But what if I wear shoes, although I do hate them. And I could wear a hat even and gloves, if you think it's too...'

'No!' the woman snapped. 'What did I tell you?'

Etta's heart sank, 'It's for my own good, I know...' She looked longingly out of the window.

'What else did I tell you?' the woman had her hands on her hips.

Uh-oh. Time to be a good girl now.

'Things always happen for a reason and there is always a good reason for everything,' Etta parroted diligently.

Like locked doors and windows. If it weren't for those she'd have climbed out at night and explored those sheds to her heart's content.

'Precisely,' the woman said, 'You're the only one out of...'

'Only one out of whom?' Etta got curious.

The woman looked at her strangely, '...You're the only one I have interesting conversations with, so let's keep it that way, shall we?' she asked and Etta nodded. 'Now, about quantum physics...' the woman said and Etta tried to listen, which was difficult on account of the nagging questions at the back of her mind.

Chapter 3. The Toad

Etta woke to someone's heavy breathing. She lay still, hoping that whoever it was would go away and breathe somewhere else.

A couple of wheezes later, Etta was still lying still.

No such luck.

Maybe scaring would work?

Etta coughed theatrically, sat up straight and came nose-to-nose with two huge yellow eyes. A mountain of muddy bulbous flesh towered over her.

A toad!

There was a huge toad in the room!

Etta squeaked, pressed her back against her headboard and pulled the rose-leaf covers to her nose.

There was nowhere to run and only her bed to hide.

For a second there was silence.

Then there was...

'Ribbit!'

At least the wheezy breathing had stopped.

'Well, aren't you the prettiest thang!' the toad croaked. 'Ribbit!'

'How would you know? I'm hiding,' Etta mumbled.

'I watched you sleep for a long, long while,' the toad said.

Creepy.

'Never seen such a dainty thing in my life and I've seen plenty, believe me, girl,' the toad said. 'Ribbit! My baby will surely like you for a bride, yes indeed!' it croaked.

Her baby? As in her son? There were two toads in the room?!?

Before she knew it, Etta was airborne, clinging to the walls of her walnut for dear life.

Poof! went the rose petal that had served as her covers.

Etta watched her mattress of violet petals hopping across the edge of her walnut one after another.

The old toad was abducting her!

Not to marry her off straight away, Etta hoped.

When the hopping stopped, Etta held on to the walls of her bedchamber a little while longer.

Just in case.

When five minutes had passed and nothing happened, Etta's curiosity got the better of her.

She peeked.

What she saw took her breath away.

Forget the old woman's lake on the plate!

Water stretched in every direction Etta looked and a couple of water-lily islands beckoned yonder.

This was a real lake!

She spied two huge yellow eyes next to the green leaf under her walnut.

She ducked back and tried hard to contain her excitement.

How do I get her to leave me alone? Maybe if I pretend I'm afraid of water.

Etta did a few practice sobs and stabbed herself in the eye with her finger.

When she peeked out next, both her eyes were red and watering.

'Noooooo!' she whimpered at the two yellow eyes.

'Ribbit!'

'Please, let me go, please?' Etta whimpered, rubbing her eyes. 'I....I'm afraid of water...' she stage-whispered.

'Ribbit!'

The two mountains with the eyes rose a bit higher, revealing fat pink lips on yellow bulbous flesh.

Etta tried hard to contain her disgust.

'Will you marry my son?' the toad flapped her lips.

What, no preliminaries, straight to the main point of the negotiations? as the old woman would say.

Out loud, Etta whimpered, 'How can I think of marriage when I'm afraid for my life?'

'Oh, stop it. Water will do you no harm!' the toad said, 'It's lovely.'

'You know how to swim and I don't, so if I were to fall in, there would be harm. For me!' Etta said and pouted.

'Then don't fall in,' the toad said.

The eyes started sinking.

Before the lips disappeared, they said, 'Water is also calming. You shall stay here and calm down. When you're calm and no longer afraid for your life, then you'll think of marriage. And when I come back perhaps you'll have a different answer for me...'

As if!

The water gurgled and gulped and then there was silence.

Finally!

Etta shivered. For once she was glad the old woman's reprimands over Etta sleeping in her day clothes had fallen on deaf ears.

3. 'Ribbit!'

Chapter 4. The Fishes

Etta was sunning herself on her lily leaf, enjoying the quiet and the gentle rocking.

The toad had been right.

The water WAS very calming.

She yawned and stood up.

Right!

Time to get rescued.

In the fairy-tales the old woman used to read to her before bedtime, someone always came to the rescue of someone in need.

She was in need.

Surely, there was a rescuer somewhere at hand?

All she had to do was get noticed.

Sunning herself in the open hadn't worked.

Air rescue was out.

How about coast guard?

Etta walked over to the edge of the leaf and sat down, gathering her skirts so they wouldn't get wet.

She carefully slipped her feet into the water.

Ooh, nice and cold.

A welcome respite after the scorching sun.

Etta dangled her legs.

If this was a lake or a pond - which was where water-lilies grew - then there should be...

There was a splash and something nudged Etta's left foot.

Or rather someone.

'Hello!' the fish said. Several more popped their heads out to stare at Etta.

'Hello,' Etta waved. 'I'm glad I'm not alone out here!' she said.

'We heard no crying,' the fish said and its brethren nodded.

Yes, I was enjoying myself too much. 'Were you supposed to?' Etta asked.

Two black bug-eyes blinked in response.

'We heard no crying,' the fish repeated.

Oooh-kay.

'I was in shock...?' Etta suggested. 'The toad had just carried me off and left me here without food and...'

The fish nodded. 'We only knew someone was up here when you put your feet in the water,' the fish interrupted her. 'Otherwise, we would have come sooner.'

Ooh-kay.

Out loud Etta said, 'You're very helpful!' And added 'Thank you!'

The fish nodded again.

'Do you want me to bite the stem now, just like...?' the fish fell silent.

'Just like what?' Etta asked.

'Do you want me to bite the stem or not?' the fish asked testily.

'If you bite the stem, the lily will...'

'Drift, yes,' the fish said and Etta nodded.

That meant there was an undercurrent in this body of water.

'In that case, yes please,' she said, not knowing where the drifting would get her, but hopefully away from where the toad had left her. She hoped the undercurrent would carry her far far away.

Who knew when the toad mama would be coming back to check if Etta had changed her mind to marry 'her baby'.

'Is there any way I could get a morsel of food, please? Fresh water I have,' Etta gestured around her. 'All I need is a little...'

'Talk to the butterfly,' the fish said and dived. Moments later Etta noticed her surroundings had slightly shifted. The lilies that were once far seemed closer and brighter.

She was on the move! Yay!

'Butterfly, what butterfly?' Etta mumbled and raised her hand to her eyes.

A shadow obliterated the sun.

Whoosh!

Whoosh!

Whoosh!

Etta noticed two giant white stripes moving toward and away from her.

'Hello! May I sit down, please?' a tiny voice asked from above.

'Oh, yes, sure, if you'll fit,' Etta said and stepped into her walnut.

Who knew what area the giant thing would occupy? Let's just hope it doesn't sink the leaf!

'The thing' swooped down and elegantly folded its huge blue wings. The leaf hardly wobbled. 'Hi, I'm Annabel,' said the butterfly.

'Hi, I'm Etta,' Etta said. 'You look...you look lovely,' she said and reached out to touch the white stripe.

'Thank you, Etta. Do you want to fasten me to your leaf so I can carry you far far away from here?' Annabel asked and Etta noticed two silk threads hanging from the butterfly's neck.

'Yes, please. But first, can we get something to eat?' Etta asked.

Chapter 5. The Butterfly

When Etta had had her fill of the pollen that Annabel had shared with her, she patted her belly and took the reins. 'Now, we fly?' she asked.

Annabel looked startled, 'We? What do you mean we? I fly, not we.'

Semantics, as the old woman would say. Out loud, Etta said, 'Of course, I meant no disrespect, you fly and I sit on your back, so technically I don't fly and we don't fly, but I fly with you. On your back. Right?' she asked, sensing Annabel's hesitation.

'I don't know...' Annabel shifted away from Etta so the silk reins slipped through Etta's fingers.

'Well, what did you have in mind?' Etta asked, praying the butterfly was not skittish and wouldn't take off immediately.

'Well, I was told that you should fasten the threads to the leaf and I would pull it,' Annabel said.

'Told by whom?' Etta asked.

'You don't know them,' Annabel shrugged.

'Yes, but who are 'they'?' Etta wouldn't let it go.

'What does it matter? If I told you their names, that is just useless information because I don't think you'd ever meet them. Nor should you want to,' the butterfly shivered. 'Now, do you want to get away from here or not?' she asked.

'Sure, let's! So I need to fasten these threads to...' Etta asked.

'The stem of the lily leaf,' Annabel finished helpfully. 'I hope the fishes haven't chewed it all up like...' the butterfly fell silent, '...like I know that they sometimes can.'

'How do you know that they sometimes can?' Etta asked.

'Aren't you an inquisitive one,' Annabel said. 'Now fasten me to your leaf and let's go. Before the toad returns,' she added.

'You know about the toad?' Etta asked.

'You told me about her, didn't you?' Annabel fluttered her eyelashes.

No, she really hadn't.

'How do you know it's a her?' Etta asked instead, finding the stem and fastening the threads.

'I think I see the toad, let's go,' Annabel exclaimed and off she went, jerking the leaf in the process.

Etta almost fell head-first into the water and grabbed her walnut to steady herself.

'Hey, gently!' she yelled, but either the butterfly didn't hear her or didn't want to hear her.

Some rescue. If she didn't know how to swim, she could have fallen overboard for all the butterfly seemed to care.

Still, they were moving. Fast.

***

Half a day later, Etta was getting bored. They had criss-crossed what seemed to be a pond and Annabel hadn't found any bit of shore suitable enough for a landing. Instead, her butterfly had landed on her leaf for a brief pitstop.

'Now, shall we try the southern shore, Annabel?' Etta said for the fifth time, hoping for a different answer. 'Why you are avoiding that direction is beyond me,' she added.

'I'm avoiding it because I know there is nothing there,' Annabel said.

'And you know this how?' Etta asked.

'On my way here, I flew from that direction and I'm telling you, there was nothing there. Nothing good, anyway,' the butterfly fluttered her wings.

'Ok, nothing good, but what's so bad that you don't want to go there? Maybe what's not good for you might just as well turn out to be good for me?' Etta asked.

'I don't think so. Please. Don't ask, just believe me. Please.' Annabel was quite serious.

Ok, she's definitely hiding something.

'By the way, why did you fly this way?' Etta asked.

'What's that?' Annabel pretended not to understand.

'Why did you happen to fly this way? I'm just curious whether it was blind luck or something else that made you fly this way, find me and offer to help me,' Etta asked, tried to bat her eyelashes and didn't succeed.

Annabel thought about it, 'Blind luck?' she offered.

'Fine, don't tell me,' Etta threw up her hands. 'Sooner or later I'll find out anyway,' she said, hoping she would.

Especially if Annabel cracked now.

Annabel folded her wings. 'Our pit-stop is over,' she said and ascended, leaving Etta grabbing at the walnut shell for balance again.

When Etta ascertained that they were going north again, she sighed.

Argh!

This was no different than rowing on the old woman's plate for years and years!

Luckily for her butterflies didn't live that long, so Annabel would have to pick where to land sometime.

Hopefully today.

Five minutes later, she heard a small aeroplane approaching. At least that's the sound she remembered from the very few war movies the old woman had watched with her. The old woman hated war movies in general and on principle.

The sound kept getting louder and louder. Etta eyed the skies.

No plane.

4. *'Hi, I'm Annabel!'*

Instead, a shiny tiny dark dot was getting closer and closer, zig-zagging as if unable to follow a straight line.

When it was directly above them, the dot dived at Etta.

She screamed and ran for her walnut, although there was no violet leaf mattress nor rose petal covers to hide under any more.

The deafening buzzing stopped.

The thing had landed so softly that it didn't deter Annabel on her stubborn one-way journey.

Etta peeked out and saw a bug preening its antlers.

'Hello! Who are you?' she asked.

The preening stopped. 'Uh, hello, yes, well, here you are and here I am and…I'm Stephen,' the bug said, puffed out his chest and fluttered his grey-orange wings.

'Those are beautiful,' Etta said despite her fright and reached out her hand.

'Oh, you like my wings?' Stephen asked.

'Yes, very much. How did you get them?' Etta asked.

'I was born with them. We all are,' Stephen said.

'You all?' Etta asked.

'Cockchafers,' the bug said, 'May bugs in common vernacular,' he added, straightening his posture.

'Oh,' Etta said.

'Do you want to see where I live?' Stephen asked. 'Meet other bugs with even more beautiful wings than mine?'

'There are even more beautiful wings than yours?' Etta was amazed and Stephen nodded. 'Oh…alright.'

She could spare the time for a visit. Annabel would still be traversing this pond when she got back.

'Where do you live?' Etta asked.

The bug pointed in the direction opposite to where the butterfly-drawn leaf was headed.

South.

They'd be flying south.

The bug tossed her the reins that Etta had mistaken for his long dandy scarf and patted his flank.

Wow, all the insects here seemed to come really well equipped for humanoid transportation.

'Hop on and let's go!' Stephen ordered. 'I can't wait for my kin to meet the most gorgeous girl I've ever laid my eyes on,' the two black peas on his head bulged even more.

'Thank you! At least let me say goodbye and let my butterfly know when I will be back!' Etta laughed as the buzzing started literally in her ears. 'By the way, when shall we be back?' she yelled.

'Why should we go back?' the bug threw over his shoulder, ascending over the reeds.

Suddenly, a vast body of water was roaring beneath them.

This riverbank infested with reeds turned out to be hiding a rocky river!

'To untie the butterfly!' Etta yelled pointing below at the adrift leaf weaving its way after Annabel.

Although if Annabel had known about the bigger body of water and refused to help her, Etta was tempted not to help her either.

Stephen shrugged in response and continued his flight.

They rose higher and the roar subsided, giving way to a peaceful view of a snaking body of water below.

A river!

Annabel had been getting them lost in just one nook of a river?

Still, she had saved her from the toad.

The least Etta could do was make sure she was free to continue on her way.

'Listen, I do want to go with you to see where you live, but then one of your kin will have to untie the butterfly. Please?' Etta pleaded with the May bug.

'Absolutely!' Stephen assured her without a backwards glance.

Such certainty could only mean that Stephen had thought about everything before he had picked her up.

That's what he must have meant when he had said there was no point in going back.

What admirable foresight!

'Oh, you have arranged someone to fly in to take care of it already?' Etta yelled.

'Absolutely!' said the May bug.

'Oh, thank you! Thank you! Thank you!' Etta yelped and pressed herself to Stephen's back.

The bug stiffened for a second and then relaxed again, aiming for the tiny oak tree in the distance, past which the river snaked.

5. *'I'm Stephen.'*

Chapter 6. The May Bugs

Etta didn't get to admire the scenery for very long. Colourful meadows with strange flowers dotted the river's banks. Etta did make out her favourite red tulips, spotting daisies, daffodils, callas and forget-me-nots in colours she had never seen before - pink, turquoise, orange and peach. Sometimes Etta couldn't distinguish whether it was just fresh soil or vegetation so purple it seemed black.

And then there was the river.

The way it glistened in the sun reminded Etta of conversations she had had with her old woman about the properties of light and water. To a common eye, the river seemed toad-green, but that was just the vegetation underneath the surface. *Water*, Etta remembered, *was like air - no colour, no taste, no smell.*

At least pure water.

The water in the pond had been drinkable, but a bit smelly. There was a twangy taste of decaying vegetation, which was weird, because if the pond was really a nook of the river, then the supply of fresh water should have kept that nook fresh as well.

The river...the river...

The river Annabel knew was there and refused to travel along.

It made Etta wonder why.

She remembered the rule the old woman had reminded her of time and again.

Things always happen for a reason and there is always a good reason for everything.

The old woman seldom smiled when she parroted that rule.

Etta had always suspected the things that had happened to the old woman and the reasons they had happened were probably not good ones.

I mean, who would go to a witch to get a child?

Well, for fifteen years, the old woman got what she had paid for.

Etta.

All of a sudden, the bug's buzzing became feverish.

Even if the flight wasn't long, it was sufficiently strenuous for Stephen. He had started huffing and puffing like the toy choo-choo train the old woman had sometimes wound up when she had thought Etta was asleep.

Etta swallowed to keep her ears open.

Stephen was descending.

Onto the oak tree, tiny no longer.

As they approached the kingly crown of the leafy giant, Etta tried to imagine what Stephen's kin and home would be like. If all May bugs were as kind to strangers as Stephen had been, and made her feel right at home, maybe she could live with them? Unless she could persuade Stephen to take her back to the old woman...

They landed in front of a gathering of buzzing bugs.

A welcoming committee?

Ooh, this looked like fun!

'Hello, I'm Etta and I'm so pleased to meet Stephen's family!' she said dismounting Stephen who was dabbing at his forehead with a handkerchief.

'What's this?' one of the larger bugs said.

Who, not what Etta mentally corrected it.

'This...is...what did you say your name was, pretty girl?' Stephen asked.

Etta smiled. *Yes, of course, they had sped away in such a hurry that...no wait, she HAD given him her name, hadn't she?* 'Etta, I'm Etta...' she said.

'This is what they grow up to be?' another bug asked and stepped up to Etta, inspecting her.

Etta hid behind Stephen.

Stephen stepped aside and gestured, 'Etta, meet everyone. Everyone, meet Etta,' he said.

Maybe he didn't understand she was afraid?
Maybe he didn't think she should be afraid of his kin?
Maybe they are all just a bit gruff?

Etta straightened up and opened her arms wide - *nice, open gestures, like the woman had taught her* - and asked 'Which one of you do I thank for untying my butterfly?'

The May bugs eyed her warily.

'Fui, she makes such hideous sounds! Quite different from our sweet buzzing, brother,' one said.

'I'm sorry if my voice offends you. Or perhaps you're tired of waiting for my words of gratitude. Was it you who untied my butterfly?' Etta asked and approached the bug who had critiqued her voice. The bug just turned away.

'Fui! How ugly her gait is! How clumsily she walks on only two legs!' Another bug snickered.

'And look at the fat sausages at the end of her upper feelers, ugh!' Another bug chimed in.

Etta's smile faded as she looked about, confused.

'The only pretty thing about her, brother, are her eyes,' someone said and Etta turned to the bug, smiling in exchange for its words of kindness. 'But they could be bigger and darker and on her forehead. I mean, you can hardly see them!'

Etta's smile evaporated altogether.

If they were so unkind to their guests, Etta feared for the complete strangers that crossed their path.

Dread started creeping up her spine, 'Please tell me, did any of you untie my butterfly?' she asked, her voice slightly shaking. 'You did ask someone to do that, Stephen, didn't you?' Etta pleaded.

Silence was her answer.

'Nobody helped her? Annabel is still tied up to the leaf? Unable to get away?' Etta looked around.

The bugs just stood there. Some looked bored.

Etta felt her hands clench into fists.

Stephen had the good sense to look embarrassed.

'You knew it couldn't untie itself! You knew! And you didn't send anyone to help? How could you! You promised!' Etta's tiny fists drummed against the bug's chest.

'I said nothing of the sort!' Stephen protested and carefully distanced himself from Etta.

'You said 'Absolutely!' I remember that!' Etta said, feeling the sobs starting.

'I always say 'absolutely' to requests from pretty maidens. Sometimes they slip my mind, but the maidens always remind me if it's really important,' the bug said.

'Life or death is not sufficiently important for you to remember the request the first time?' Etta was aghast.

'Not if it's not my life or death,' the bug shrugged. 'We were flying, remember? I had no way to communicate with anyone here mid-flight. Besides, we have no fingers, how would any of us be able to untie the butterfly? You assumed too much and you yourself condemned the poor thing to death,' Stephen said.

Etta blinked back tears.

She felt sorry.

For herself.

For Annabel.

For Stephen.

The worst part was, Stephen wasn't wrong.

Every word coming out of his jaws was horribly correct.

How could she have been so irresponsible?

Leaving someone else to do what she should have done.

Believing someone would simply oblige because it made sense.

Because she had asked nicely.

How could she have been so naive to believe that if someone did right by her, they were a do-gooder through and through?

How could she have been so foolish?

It was all her fault.

But the bug could have said something at the time!

He could have said no.

Instead, he had said 'Absolutely!' and she had stopped thinking about it since with that word it had become someone else's problem.

Except that it hadn't.

The bugs, they could have done something.

Instead, they had done nothing!

'You have mouths with very sizable jaws! You could have snapped the silk threads linking the butterfly and the leaf!' Etta shrieked, her hands flying to her mouth.

How very unladylike, is what the old woman would have said.

Oh, fiddlesticks! The old woman never felt such helpless rage over such incredible disregard for other living beings!

'I don't see a point in continuing this academic discussion. And with such an ugly specimen!' One of the larger bugs said. 'Stephen, get rid of her!' It ordered and Etta briefly wondered if 'getting rid of her' meant that those sizable jaws were about to clasp around her neck in the very near future.

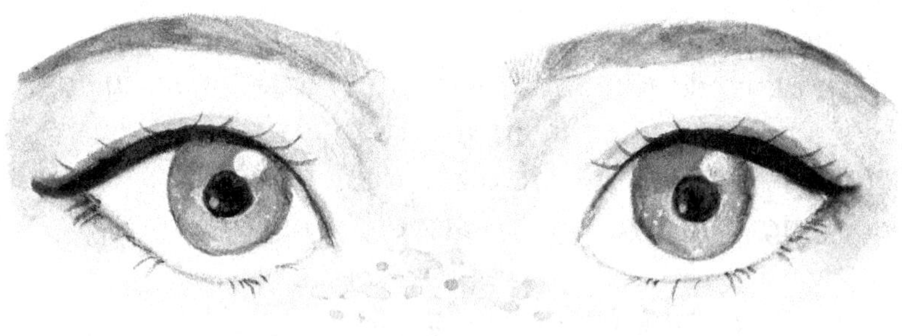

6. *'The only pretty thing about her, brother,
are her eyes.'*

***

When all the bugs, even Stephen, turned on her, Etta pretended to faint.

Fainting is always a good trick when you don't know what else to do, she remembered the old woman saying.

Now, she was being held fast between Stephen's sizable jaws and by the feel of it, they were descending.

Well, it's a good thing they didn't decide to just throw me down.

Maybe there is hope for these mean bugs after all.

Since there was no imminent threat to her life and the deafening buzzing was also somehow gently lulling, Etta's mind wandered.

Why had she taken Annabel's word that she must tie her to the leaf? If she had persuaded Annabel to fly the two of them away, she would never have ended up with the bugs.

If Annabel had continued to be stubborn, she could have asked her to stop somewhere, anywhere, and then she could have thanked Annabel and journeyed onward alone.

Except she didn't know the terrain and maybe she would have ended up back with the toad.

Ugh.

Etta shuddered.

Who knew what the toad would do, if she refused to marry her son.

Eat her?

Drown her?

Surely NOT deposit her back to the old woman's house.

If the toad was callous enough to leave her stranded in the middle of a pond without food, she would probably not return things to the way they were if she didn't get her own way.

Marriage.

To a toad.

Etta shuddered again.

The old woman had been married once.

She hardly ever spoke of it, but Etta had gathered that getting married was somewhat of a preoccupation for the human females.

And not only the human females, if the toad was anything to go by.

Stephen started making the feverish pitched sound again and then there was the softest touch down Etta could have imagined.

The bug laid her gently on a freshly fallen leaf.

He stood there silently and sighed heavily a few times.

'I've always wanted to know how you girls would turn out when you're all grown up. Now I know. You truly are beautiful. I'm sorry I cannot keep you. I really, really would, if I could, but I doubt that either SHE or THEM would allow me to, you know.'

One regretful sigh later Stephen was gone.

When the buzzing grew distant, Etta squinted her eyes open.

She saw ferns. Lots and lots of ferns.

I'll wait until the buzzing stops and then I'll scamper off.

If trees and flowers can live here, so can I.

In the course of the next few days Etta found out she could live in the forest very well indeed, all thanks to the old woman's wilderness and kitchen survival and mountaineering challenges.

Etta found out that she knew quite a few edible plants, berries and flowers. As long as she got up early enough to gather dew, food and water was taken care of.

She even got accustomed to the forest descending into mute darkness at night, a silence so eerie she kept watch the first few nights until sleep got the best of her.

As she got more and more accustomed to her surroundings one thing became clear.

While she figured out what to do next, she'd have to make herself a home.

A temporary one.

With dread, Etta remembered the old woman saying that it was the temporary things that ended up lasting the longest.

7. The oak tree, tiny no longer.

Chapter 7. The Forest

In the two weeks that Etta had lived in the woods she had not found a single living being. It seemed that nobody lived here besides the May bugs and her, which was absurd.

The woods the old woman had read to her about were always full of animals and birds and bugs and crawling things.

Snakes!

That's what the old woman had called them. Etta had a vivid recollection of a story the old woman had read her where a particularly big and nasty snake had swallowed a man whole while he had slept. Well, paralysed him with its venom or strangled him and then swallowed him, but swallowed him nevertheless.

Not that she particularly wanted to be swallowed whole, which is was why she had kept watch the first few nights she had spent in the woods before finding a hollow she had adopted as a home.

Well, the eerie mute darkness had kept her up as well.

During the day, there were birds up in the trees. Some tweeted and sang, but they never came down to her level and the weirdest thing was - she never saw them fly.

It was as if light awoke them and darkness cowered everyone into silence.

Etta remembered the old woman playing her the sounds of nightly owl calls.

Maybe there were no owls in this part of the woods?

So far she hadn't SEEN a single bird.

Maybe there were no real birds up in those trees?

What if there were just...

Sounds?

What had the old woman called them? Audio something. Tapes? Tracks? Songs?

Neither had she seen a single animal paw print on the ground.

Not a single one.

She had turned nocturnal for a few days, hoping against hope the forest would somehow come to life at night.

She heard and saw nothing at night.

Nothing.

A quiet dark forest was especially creepy.

If the light seemed to switch things on, the darkness seemed to switch everything off.

If it hadn't been for the May bugs, she would have proclaimed this neck of the woods to be completely abandoned.

At least things grew here, so it wasn't a dead zone.

She had berries and plants, mushrooms and sap to choose from, so she never went hungry.

She even had fire for cooking. One lovely midday she found a drying patch of grass that started to smoke under her very eyes. She found some twigs and figured out how to keep the fire going in a fragment of a clay pot she had stumbled upon.

The clothes on her back were wearing a bit thin and that made her miss her wonderful wardrobe full of dresses and pantsuits at the old woman's house.

Etta gathered up her few belongings - a flask she had made out of an oak leaf and a cone for her berries.

It was time to head home.

The oak leaf was an old one she had collected from near the tree where the May bugs lived. Etta shuddered, remembering their hospitality. She didn't fancy running into the May bugs again.

Nobody was that lonely.

Their constant buzzing was a live beacon that helped Etta avoid them as well as find her way to her cosy tree hollow each night.

Chapter 8. The Mouse

It was a good thing that Etta had become used to talking toads, fishes, butterflies and bugs, because when she spied a mouse walking around on its hind legs, this no longer struck her as strange.

The critter perked up and wriggled its whiskers.

Had it heard her?

The mouse dashed about doing some weird zig-zags and then hopped into a small hole in a tree. The same tree under which Etta had found the clay pot. Now she knew to whom the pot belonged.

She didn't know whether she was happy that she was no longer alone.

Who knew if the critter was even sentient?

It could very well be that she still had no one to talk to.

A few days later Etta passed the mouse's tree again and spied that the small hole had been boarded up with twigs.

The mouse was building a nest. Maybe that's what mice did?

Suddenly, a side door Etta hadn't spotted opened and the mouse peeked out.

It probably was sentient, Etta decided. If the wooden door with a knocker didn't give it away, the night cap and the apron the mouse was wearing sure did.

Chapter 9. The Leaf

Etta lifted a fern and peeked.

She could hear the river.

It was close.

She spotted a lily leaf and saw an outline of a beautiful huge wing.

Annabel.

Maybe the butterfly was still alive after two weeks, just helplessly tethered to the...

The wind blew and the wing fluttered like a flag on a pole.

Half a wing.

Still attached to the drying leaf.

It was all her fault.

Etta approached the leaf to face her greatest act of recklessness.

She should have untied the butterfly before she was airborne.

Most importantly, she shouldn't have blindly trusted others to do her job.

The death of a creature that had been kind and helpful to her in her hour of need was a heavy burden she would now have to bear.

Except...

Except...

Except this wing was yellow.

Annabel's wings were blue with white stripes and black edges.

Renewed hope pushed Etta to search further along the river bank.

It wasn't long before she found another lily leaf.

And another.

Then a stack of them piled up high.

Heaps and heaps of lily leaves.

Some were withered, others fresh. Most had pretty ribbons tethered to them that looked almost festive in the breeze.

Pink, yellow, blue, white.

Etta looked around and shuddered.

There was nothing festive about this place.

This was a graveyard.

The ribbons were all remnants of wings.

She found one quantum of solace.

The only leaf with a blue ribbon was too withered to possibly be hers.

Chapter 10. There's Always a Prince

Etta woke to complete silence.

No bugs buzzing.

No birds chirping.

No ferns rustling in the wind.

Complete silence in a forest was always alarming.

Complete silence when there was light was even more alarming.

She climbed out of her window that also served as her door.

The May bugs started buzzing somewhere up high.

Well, at least someone was ok.

Against her better judgement Etta wandered over to the giant oak that she had been avoiding like the plague for weeks now.

She stumbled over a tree root and fell nose-to-nose with a sleeping girl her own size.

Glad she had finally found someone of her own species Etta said, 'Oh, hello!'

The girl didn't respond.

'Are you asleep?' Etta rolled her eyes. 'Well, get up then! Something's going on in the forest and I wouldn't want to be out in the open when the stampede starts, if I were you,' she said, crouched and shook the sleeping girl by her shoulder.

There was something unnatural in the way the girl's head rolled freely. The angles were all wrong.

Etta leaned closer and felt her wrist.

Still warm, but no pulse.

Etta looked up.

The girl had probably fallen to her death from the tree mere minutes ago.

That's why the May bugs had gone quiet.

Etta looked at the girl and suddenly everything made sense.

The May bugs knew.

Hell, the May bugs were to blame!

Etta heard a flutter of wings and hid behind a fern.

'I notified you as soon as it happened, Your Majesty,' said one of the May bugs, promptly sinking into a deep bow and Etta recognised Stephen.

Your Majesty?

As in a queen?

A winged fairy in a floor-length mossy hooded gown landed next to the dead girl and crouched, her back to where Etta was hiding. 'Such a pity. She was perhaps the prettiest fairy of them all,' she said, her voice a tinkle of a thousand tiny bells.

Fairies?

Etta clasped her hand over her mouth, stifling a gasp.

'Alas, it seems that she suffered from low self-esteem about her looks - if she killed herself after your goading. Unless you tell me she slipped,' the lady tilted her head at Stephen and folded her wings away with a snap.

No matter how Etta tried, she couldn't see the fairy queen's face as it was obscured by the hood. She crept closer.

'No, Your Majesty, she stepped off quite willingly,' Stephen said.

What had they said to the poor girl that she had wanted to kill herself?

The queen nodded and turned slightly, so that her back was still to Etta who was practically nose-to-nose with the corpse again. All Etta could see now was the embroidered slip under the queen's green dress and her dainty slippers. 'It's a pity. Such a waste...And no use to me at all... Only because you May bugs can't help yourself when it comes to your favourite pastime of goading every fairy you meet.'

Clearly, the lady had already decided whom to blame.

Wait, did the lady say 'goading EVERY fairy you meet'?

Etta looked at the dead girl.

The dead girl had no wings, but if Etta wasn't mistaken, they had just called her a fairy.

But in all the fairy-tales the old woman had ever read to her fairies had wings!

Apparently, in real life, wings were optional.

Etta remembered her own run-in with the bugs and felt something at the pit of her stomach.

The old woman had never said...

Could she be a fairy?

Ignoring the bug who bent his head lower, the fairy queen shook her head, 'Now I'll have to find another failure to stand-in as the Enchantress to tame a beast or else have to curse the boy myself...'

That sounded a bit familiar, but Etta couldn't quite follow how the lady's other problems were more important than the one at hand.

A dead girl, hello?

'If it may please Your Majesty...' Stephen said and bowed even lower.

The lady waved for the bug to rise, 'Oh, stop grovelling. You were only doing what I tasked you to do.'

The fairy queen had actually tasked the May bugs to goad lonely young fairies to suicide over their looks?

'You are such a powerful enchantress, Your Majesty. You simply cannot squander your precious time on standing in as a common fairy in other fairy-tales...' the May bug said.

'Enchantresses are hardly common,' she said, absent-mindedly toeing the dead girl with her embroidered slipper, 'What are you proposing?' The queen enquired, straightening her robes.

Etta remembered the CSI episodes she had used to watch with the older woman.

Where was the coroner?

With royalty and bugs in deep conversation about themselves, no one was paying any attention to the remains of the unfortunate girl right in front of them.

'Perhaps you could revive her? I'm sure with your magic it is quite feasible.' The bug offered.

'Feasible doesn't necessarily mean it should be done,' the queen bit off.

'If she is lost to this fairy-tale, maybe she could still be useful in another one? Exactly as you had planned?' The bug said. 'Nobody would be able to tell there that she is one of the walking dead. And you wouldn't have to lower yourself to stand in as an Enchantress.'

'Instead, you would have me use dark magic,' the lady said.

The bug looked at her slyly, 'How is your scheme with the orphans different from using dark magic?' The bug whispered and noticing the queen's wand hand twitch added 'I just don't understand, that's all, Milady, forgive me for being stupid.'

Etta listened breathlessly.

'The scheme is for the greater good,' the queen said, sounding defensive.

'This would be too,' the bug reassured her.

After a moment's hesitation, the lady hovered over the dead girl, her hood still hiding her face. She leaned in, tapped the girl's chest with her wand and whispered something.

Etta squished her eyes shut as if that would make her invisible. She held her breath and listened very intently.

Who knew, it might come in handy one day. If ever she had a wand and wings and needed to revive someone.

'*Resumo. Rescindo. Vitam ago.*'

The girl drew a breath, opened her eyes and sat up, dead no more.

'Oh, hello!' the resurrected corpse said to the not-so-innocent bystanders. 'I had quite a fall,' she looked up at the tree, the top of which was miles away, 'I hope I didn't hurt anyone when I...when I...' she mumbled.

'...Landed,' the lady finished helpfully.

'Yes,' the girl turned pale as she noticed Stephen. 'Oh...it's you... What else do you want from me?' she asked as her face crumpled.

'Nothing,' Stephen huffed and flew off.

'Now,' the lady said kindly and helped the girl up. 'It's such an excellent thing that I ran into you,' the queen said.

'It is?' the girl asked.

'Yes, absolutely. I need your help, dear. Will you help me? A pretty girl such as yourself is most surely also kind,' the lady said.

With the bully gone, the girl visibly relaxed, 'Of course. How may I help?' She asked.

'Would you like to travel to distant lands and punish those who think beauty can only be skin deep?'

Etta saw the girl blink in surprise.

Yep, I'd be surprised too, to get an amazing travelling offer five seconds after meeting someone.

Meanwhile, the fairy queen continued, 'Where there are beings who believe that kindness and good intentions don't count at all? Who only measure the worth of others by how alike they are to them in terms of looks or status?' The lady asked, her chin rising.

Wow, a bit of an oversell? Etta thought and watched the girl's mouth drawing into a fine line.

'Yes, yes I would,' the undead girl whispered, glancing up at where the May bugs were still buzzing.

Wow, oversell sold...apparently.

'Then I have just the job for you!' The lady beamed.

'What do I have to do?' the girl asked.

'You would have to pretend to be an ugly old hag...mind you, only pretend,' the lady hastened to add when she saw the girl recoil, 'and after a very brief conversation you will reveal yourself to the prince to be the most beautiful and powerful Enchantress...'

'There's a prince?' the girl asked.

'There's a prince,' the lady nodded.

Etta thought about the fairy-tales she knew and loved.

There's always a prince.

'Just stay here while I...arrange things and I will come back for you, with proper clothes fit for a princess and a spell-book since Enchantresses always have spell-books...and upon my return we shall go together to a lovely new land. Would you like that?' the lady asked and the girl nodded. 'You'll be alright by yourself for a couple of hours, won't you?' She asked. 'You can dream of the prince who will surely be in awe of your beauty once he sees you,' the queen said and flitted away, leaving not one but two fairies slack-jawed.

8.   Enchantresses always have spell-books.

***

Etta had a hard time deciding whether she should reveal herself. Something in the fairy queen's proposition did not seem right.

Especially since she knew what the May bugs were up to. She had tasked them to do it!

That lady was up to no good.

Her kind intentions were hard to believe, particularly after that bout of callousness she had exhibited when she had discovered that the girl was dead.

Etta decided the resurrected fairy could use a fair warning.

'Psst!' She said and hoped the girl was not prone to screaming.

The undead fairy slash future Enchantress turned around, sitting as she was. 'Oh, hello! I didn't realise someone else was here!' She clasped her hands in delight. 'Oh, how lovely! I'm Caroline. What's your name?'

'Etta,' said Etta and crouched by Caroline. 'You're quite lucky, you know.'

'Yes, I do know! Imagine, such good luck running into my fairy godmother...'

'Fairy godmother?' Etta asked, 'Are you sure that's who she is?'

'I mean who else could she possibly be, if she is arranging for me to meet my prince straight away...' Caroline blushed. 'Mind you, in exchange for a few minutes of being ugly,' the girl shuddered. 'Although even a few minutes are much too much, but I guess that's fair...'

'Did she actually say YOU were the one the prince was meant to...wed?' Etta asked.

'Well, no, but who else could it possibly be? A fair Enchantress meeting a prince...it's destiny, isn't it?' Caroline eyed Etta with her baby-blues.

'It could...but it could also be that you're just there to perform a service and won't necessarily get the prince as a reward,' Etta cautioned the innocent.

'Whatever do you mean?'

'She...your...fairy godmother...' Etta squeezed the words out - *she wasn't but it eased conversation* '...she wanted your help, right?' Etta asked and the girl nodded.

'Well, when is the part where you help her?' Etta asked.

'Before. Before I meet the prince. I meet him after I teach some nasty people a lesson,' the girl nodded primly. 'And you do know it's terribly impolite to eavesdrop, don't you?'

'If I hadn't eavesdropped, you wouldn't know the half of it,' Etta said.

'Half of what?' Caroline asked.

'Your story. For instance, did you know that just moments before you were lying here quite dead?' Etta hoped her knowledge would convince the girl that her point about the prince was also sound.

'What?' the fairy jumped to her feet. 'Now you're just making things up!'

'No, really, you were. You lay here, unmoving, your neck was at a funny angle and then the May bug and the queen had a bit of a talk before she revived you....' Etta rushed through the words, seeing the girl's trust evaporating.

'You're lying! You're just jealous the fairy godmother picked me to meet the prince and not you because I'm more beautiful than you are!' Caroline shouted, her face contorting with anger.

'Yeah, that grimace is particularly fetching!' Etta said. 'If you don't believe me, fine, but don't come crying, if the reality turns out to be quite different from what you think you were promised.'

'Oh, I won't, trust me!' The undead fairy stomped her foot.

'I trust you, I trust you, so it might be nice if this went both ways,' Etta mumbled.

'Just leave me alone!' Caroline yelled after her.

'Was planning to anyway!' Etta yelled back, pretending to leave but ducking back, so she could find out how this would end.

Although, if the fairy queen slash fairy godmother planned to fly Caroline somewhere, Etta had no clue how she could follow suit.

Having no wings was a serious nuisance.

Chapter 11. The Oak

Etta stared up at the oak. She was back. She didn't want to be back, she was positively tired of being back at the oak, she was sick and tired of the oak itself and yet - here she was again.

Yesterday, she had really, really tried to end up somewhere that was NOT the oak and NOT the graveyard.

It was weeks before she had noticed she was traipsing between the decay-filled river nook and the bug-infested oak.

At first, she had thought that it was just good luck that she ended up somewhere in the vicinity of the oak every single day. Her tree hollow, the mouse and pretty much everything seemed to be not too far from that tree. Etta frowned, remembering how she had cockily congratulated herself on being such a good girl scout as the old woman might say.

It wasn't until she went in search of where the queen had taken Caroline and deliberately tried NOT to get to the oak OR the river when her troubles began.

Everything was dandy, the paths leading away from the tree were scenic and lovely, the surroundings were always different, except she didn't seem to be able to get away from this place!

At all!!!

Yesterday evening, she had taken the path furthest from the river AND the tree AND she had felt she was getting further and further away, going deep into the forest. It had felt good to be finally walking away from this place, from loneliness, from everything.

Yet, here she was again.

Staring at that damned oak.

Etta retreated under the ferns to avoid being spotted by the bugs as much as to avoid seeing the cursed tree.

It seemed that whatever paths she took sooner or later circled back to the leafy giant.

The May bugs and the reclusive mouse seemed to be the only inhabitants of this patch of the woods.

Why have all these trodden paths with nobody but Etta to tread them!

How she longed to get to the colourful fields of flowers she had seen during her flight here!

Instead, all she got was the oak.

The main question she had was not how - an enchantment, clearly, as all the old woman's story-books would doubtlessly confirm - but why?

Why did someone need to enchant a specific part of the woods to circle back on itself?

So nobody would leave?

The bugs had been here before Etta had arrived.

The mouse – she had no idea. It didn't look like it was leaving, though.

Caroline had arrived afterwards...only to be whisked away by the fairy queen.

The May bugs could obviously come and go as they pleased.

So one could leave - by air.

Why did the underbrush need to be enchanted?

So whoever arrived on foot would end up by the oak, with the bugs?

While the bugs seemed to benefit by having someone to goad, she doubted they had the intelligence to conjure such powerful magic.

So, who did and where were they?

Etta doubted a wee fairy queen was that powerful, even with all her clever schemes and spell-books.

Mysteries and enchantments.

And not a wand or spell-book in sight!

Etta stomped her foot.

Fine!

Tomorrow, she would go completely off-piste as the old woman would say.

If you want different results, do something completely different, she remembered the old woman saying.

This time, she would mark the ferns and ignore the trodden paths completely and see where that would take her.

Hopefully, somewhere...different.

9. *Your Majesty?*

Chapter 12. The Hare

Trekking in the underbrush, Etta decided to check on the mouse.

The Missus' house looked more and more like a home every time Etta had passed it when searching for a way out of the woods.

Etta waited until the critter peeked out.

The mouse mumbled something and locked her door.

From the inside.

Why would a solitary mouse lock her door in the middle of the woods where nobody else lived?

The only being the mouse could have possibly sensed was Etta.

Etta left the mouse be and made her way through the ferns, trying to avoid any paths.

The aim was to get to the outmost perimeter of the forest.

Scratch that.

The aim was to get anywhere else but the oak or the butterfly graveyard.

By nightfall, Etta couldn't see the oak from near or afar.

She was close to ecstatic.

She was also dead tired.

Etta made a nest from twigs, snuggling under a fern leaf.

Sleeping out in the open made her uncomfortable, but Etta squished her eyes shut, pulled the covers up to her nose and fell asleep with a smile on her face.

She had made it as far as was possible from that damned tree.

Finally.

***

In the morning, she went to explore this new forest of ferns and birches, gathering dew and making sure she left cuts and marks to get back to where she had stayed the night.

When she emerged at her resting place a few hours later, she almost didn't believe her eyes.

The forest of grass and ferns had disappeared.

If it hadn't been for her cuts and marks, which ended here, she would be doubting her sanity.

She was looking at a meadow.

The grass was mowed, but patchily and the ferns she had carefully tied together as a make-shift shelter were nowhere to be seen.

It was as if someone had come in and chopped away half of the undergrowth.

She hid behind the remaining ferns and had to hold on for dear life when the earth shook violently.

An earthquake!

And another one!

And yet another one!

And it was getting closer!!

A brown hare hopped into view.

From afar, it didn't seem like a giant, except Etta knew that if it happened upon her, it would probably squash her and not even notice.

Ooh-kay, a bunny.

Where had it come from?

Etta heard masticating.

The crunches were like thunder.

It occurred to her that hiding in the ferns when half of them were gone was probably not a good idea.

The hare nibbled on the greener patches of longer grass and ignored the ferns.

Probably too bitter for it.

Etta exhaled.

When the giant bunny turned its nose, sniffed a few times and started hopping away, Etta followed it, ignoring the rumbling earth.

By the time the critter finally stopped, Etta was out of breath.

Bunnies, Etta thought, clasping her knees to get her breath back.

She had had to run for dear life just to keep up with it.

Etta saw the hare prepare for a hop and groaned, bracing herself for another spurt.

The hare hopped and...

Collided with...something that wasn't there.

Thrown back, it shook its ears and wriggled its nose and tried again.

And again.

Same result.

There was an invisible wall boxing the forest in?

The hare hopped helplessly to and fro alongside the freaky formation, occasionally attempting to get through without avail.

Why was she not surprised.

A long wall, by the looks of it.

Etta walked up to the hare who sniffed the air and ignored her completely.

Yes, buddy, I get it, you've got problems of your own.

She reached out toward the barrier she couldn't see until her hand touched something solid.

When she pushed against the air, the obstacle wobbled and pushed back.

Rubbery.

Etta took a step back.

She couldn't pass through this thing either.

In front of her, she saw a forest that looked a little familiar, especially that twinned birch on the right she was sure she had just passed.

Etta looked back.

The twinned birch stared back at her.
On her left.
She turned back to the wall.
Forest with the birch on the right.
She turned back to the forest.
The exact same forest with the birch on the left.
It was a mirror!
Etta turned back to inspect the wall.
A funny mirror that only reflected the forest behind her, but not Etta.
Etta glanced at the hare.
It wasn't being reflected either.
Maybe it was a looped recording, like in the movies the old woman used to show her, where the good guys recorded something for a few minutes and then connected it with the feed seen by someone else so that they wouldn't see the good guys sneaking past?
Or maybe it was a magic mirror that showed flora and inanimate objects, but not fauna?
She looked at her satchel.
Maybe objects in the hands of 'fauna' did not reflect either?
Etta stepped back and dropped her satchel.
It did not appear in the mirror.
Ok, so what she was seeing WAS a recording of what was behind her, set on loop.
She put her hand up and touched the rubbery reflective surface again.
How very...Mission Impossible.
There was an invisible wall separating...
Separating what exactly?
The hare had obviously come here from there, wherever there was. That's why it was trying to get back.
Again, the old woman was right - the grass might seem greener on the other side, but there are always consequences.
Etta patted the hare who eyed her warily.

At least there were animals on the other side of this wall.

'Having trouble getting back?' Etta shouted at the bunny's nose.

It sniffed her tentatively, but didn't say anything, it eyes darting to and fro.

'I said - did you come from over there?' Etta shouted again.

The animal wriggled its whiskers and lost interest in her.

Trying not to feel insulted, Etta eyed the wall.

Whatever it was shielding, she had learnt two important things today.

One, her enchanted part of the forest was shielded from the rest of the world by an invisible, impenetrable wall, and two, on the other side, animals lacked the power of speech.

***

When Etta woke the next day, the hare was gone.

At first, she thought it had managed to cross back somehow.

Was there a magical hour, like midnight or something, when the veil between the worlds became so thin it could hop back and she had missed it?

Scrounging the underbrush for berries, she came upon something strange.

Red dew.

A drop fell on her nose and trickled down.

She tasted it.

Salty.

Etta tried to look up through the ferns to figure out where the salty dew could have come from and waded into something doughy.

A bog in a forest of ferns?

Impossible!

She looked down.

Her bare feet were stuck in reddish brown goo.

Eeuw.

Etta noticed something was stuck to the leaves of the fern above her.

A brown tuft of something fluffy.

The colour reminded her of the hare's fur - slightly brownish with white hairs sticking out.

As the wind caught the tuft and carried it off she saw a flash of a white patch.

Etta looked down at the goo.

The bunny had left alright.

But not of its own volition.

There were no predators this side of the wall.

Something or rather someone from the other side must have caught up with it at night.

Maybe there was a good reason for the wall and for the fact that her neck of the woods was almost uninhabited?

What if the thing that ate the bunny was still here?!?

Etta backed up into the forest, away from the deathly wall.

Flee first.

Wash blood off of her feet second.

10. *Ooh-kay, a bunny.*

Chapter 13. The Fire

The next morning, Etta woke to a brook babbling nearby.

The river?

How could it be the river?

She was sure she hadn't heard it yesterday when making camp.

Etta stood up and went towards the sound.

When her feet didn't encounter roots and rocks she looked down and cursed.

A trodden path!

Somehow, despite her best efforts to stay away from them, she had ended on a path again.

And all trodden paths led back to...

The ferns parted and she found herself gazing at the graveyard.

Expecting to see the oak, Etta halted.

Wait.

All the paths led to the oak.

Right?

Except when they didn't.

Etta had trekked through the underbrush for an entire day yesterday, getting away from the invisible wall, quite sure she was NOT heading back to the oak OR the river and, most importantly, away from the deathly wall.

She had been convinced that she was finally making her escape.

By nightfall, she had decided to stop and had made a fire out in the open. She was sure she hadn't heard the river at night.

And yet, here she was.

Maybe the butterfly graveyard was somewhere in between the wall and the oak tree?

But why hadn't she heard the river at night?

Maybe the river was like the birds up in the trees?

Something that switched on and off.

Maybe there was a general switch that switched everything off?

The light, the birds, the river.

The main switch, the old woman had called it when all lights went out in her house and she had to go to the basement to switch them back on again.

Etta eyed the unkempt graveyard angrily.

Was there no escaping the usual places, no matter where she went or how she went there?

Was the entire forest enchanted?

If one were to judge by the speechless bunny and whoever had ate it, things must be different on the other side of the wall.

Maybe it was just this side of the wall, angled in by the river and the cursed oak that was enchanted.

A place with only a few players and switch-on-switch-off live decorations.

Etta sighed, toed a leaf and surveyed the decay around her.

She was surrounded by leaves at different stages of decomposition.

Etta had staked out the graveyard more than once this past month. No fresh lily leaves or butterflies had appeared since that other fairy Caroline, had died, was resurrected and taken away.

It all looked so...sad.

Etta remembered that the old woman always made a fire in her fireplace when she was feeling under the weather.

Fire!

Fire would help to clean all of this up.

Plus, maybe it would lift the enchantment?

Etta started gathering twigs.

Next, she collected the leaves and the remnants of scattered wings and heaped them high.

Then she made a tinder nest to nurture the sparks.

It was time to give all the butterflies a proper send-off.

Holding a dry twig in between her teeth, Etta smashed two flint rocks together.

Again.

And again.

And again.

When she caught a spark she blew and blew and blew at it until it became a flame which she embedded in her tinder nest and gently placed the nest under the pyre.

Now all she had to do was wait.

As a wisp of smoke snaked from the pyre, a tiny voice behind her asked 'What'cha doin'?'

Chapter 14. Willing Debtors

Etta jumped a mile and hid behind a fern. When she had caught her breath, she peeked out and saw a delicate blue butterfly, just a baby, with ornamental orange etching its wings looking around as if it was seeing everything for the first time. A cocoon with no inhabitant was lying a bit farther.

'Oh, hello! Who are you?' Etta asked.

'I'm...I'm...new,' the baby butterfly said.

'I'm Etta,' Etta said, 'I'm a fairy. You're a butterfly. Have you just hatched?'

'I believe so,' the butterfly said. 'What do butterflies do, Etta?'

'They fly!' Etta said dreamily.

'How?' The baby asked.

'They spread their beautiful wings,' she pointed at the butterfly's wings, 'and catch the wind,' Etta said.

'Can you fly?' The butterfly asked.

'Not until I have a pair of wings,' Etta sighed.

'When are you planning to grow them?' The butterfly asked.

'I don't know if I can...' Etta said.

'Who knows? Your mama?'

Etta turned sad, 'I have no mama. I'm an orphan.'

'Oh...' the butterfly said, 'Am I an orphan too?'

Two giant blue wings with black edges fanned the air, making the fire go out and the pyre scatter everywhichway. 'No, you're not. I'm your mama,' said the butterfly. 'Thank you for looking after my little one,' the mama said and fiddled her paws. 'An unusual kindness from a fairy, I must say.'

'I'm sorry. Why is it unusual for fairies to be kind?' Etta asked.

The mama butterfly fluttered its wings, 'Look around!'

'I don't understand,' Etta confessed.

'You really don't, do you?' the butterfly asked. 'It's a sad and wicked story. Are you sure that a delicate thing such as yourself wants to hear it?'

Etta nodded.

'We use this graveyard as a hatching site,' the butterfly pointed at the branches of the maple tree above them.

Etta briefly wondered about life and so much death occurring in one place.

Meanwhile, the mama butterfly was saying, '...so that our young know from the start to avoid gambling and debt.'

Gambling and debt?!?

The butterfly continued, 'Once in a while a butterfly flies too far, into the neighbouring fairy flower-colonies...'

The flowers she had seen on her way here were fairy flower-colonies?

'...and gives in to temptation. Gambling,' the mama butterfly specified and wriggled her feelers. 'Butterflies often fall into debt, and since we have no money, we have to do any task we are set to do. Mostly this involves flying across a certain area, looking to help stranded fairies.'

Etta remembered how Annabel had offered to help her without even asking why she was stranded or how she got there seconds after just meeting her.

Annabel had been making good on her gambling debts?

'The reason why I doubted your kind has any kindness in them at all is because of what you see here.' The butterfly's wings trembled. 'The butterflies who fall into debt know that they are going to an almost-certain death when they set out to help a fairy,' the mama was explaining to her newborn now. 'Because the fairies almost always forget to untie us from the lily leaves before they scamper off. And we drift with the leaf and fly until we can and when we can't birds and branches get us and we die. And fairies never even thank us for our service,' the mama added sadly.

'Are you one of the bad fairies too?' The youngling asked Etta.

'I'm afraid I might have been,' Etta said honestly. 'I didn't find my blue butterfly here,' she gestured at the pyre, 'but I still don't know what happened to Annabel because I, too, did not untie her before the May bug carried me off. I relied too much on...someone else to do what I should have done myself,' she finished sadly. 'I'm so, so sorry!' Etta said, knowing nothing she could say, least of all to a complete stranger, would ever amount to making amends.

'Did you say Annabel?' the mama butterfly asked as Etta's eyes were misting over.

***

'I did say Annabel, did you know her?' Etta asked, hoping butterflies were not the vindictive kind.

'Yes, I do know her. Everybody does. She's one of the few that got away,' mama butterfly said.

When Etta looked puzzled, the butterfly added, 'From the ungrateful fairies. Sorry, dear.'

'I'm not, since I'm the ungrateful fairy she got away from and I'm glad that she did. She's alive?' Etta asked.

'Yes. She's the president of the Veteran's club and an avid advocate against gambling, just recently married...' the mama butterfly said.

'Wow! I'm so glad to hear it!' Etta said. 'Please tell her I'm sorry if you see her, ok?' she asked.

Mama butterfly paused but nodded, while the youngling was eagerly nodding away.

'Although, you can tell her yourself, maybe? She'll be coming this way pretty soon and not just once in the coming four months,' the butterfly said.

'Four months?' Etta asked.

'She's a *Heliconius*, dear.'

When Etta looked puzzled, the mama butterfly explained, 'Feeds on pollen, lives for six months. Two months old at the moment...'

'Ahah!' was all Etta said. 'Six months, wow.'

That's short.

'Yes, that's long. Compared to the average lifespan of two weeks, that's a lot of time for flying and feeding and mating,' the mama said to her youngling.

'Are we *Heliconius...Heliconians...Heliconiuses...*' the baby spluttered.

'*Heliconii*,' Etta and the mama butterfly said in unison.

Who knew that the Latin the old woman dabbled in and tortured Etta with would come in handy in a conversation with a butterfly?

'Are we *Heliconii* too, mama?' the baby asked.

'Yes, dear, we are,' the mama said and smiled. 'We'll live a long and happy life, you and I,' she said, spreading her giant wings and motioning for them to leave.

'As long as you stay away from gambling and fairies,' Etta heard from above when the pair was already mid-flight.

Etta rolled her eyes and started gathering the remnants of butterflies and leaves back into the pyre. Being witness to new life didn't negate her self-imposed obligation to look after the dead.

Chapter 15. New Arrival

Missus Mouse had a guest.

Going by the little house had become a habit over the summer as Etta traversed the dead loop of oak-wall-graveyard-oak. Etta didn't even know why she needed to keep a tab on the mouse's doings.

Maybe after the hare, losing the only other permanent inhabitant of the enchanted wood was something she wasn't prepared to face.

En route to the wall this time, she popped by again and was glad that she had.

'I swear, girl, if you break one more thing of mine, I'm, I'm...I'm going to chase you away and winter is nigh and you know it!' she heard the mouse squeak through an open window.

'You wouldn't really turn me away, would you? I don't have anywhere else to go...' a tinkling voice said and Etta perked up.

There was a girl at the mouse's and by the sound of it she wasn't just visiting, she was living there!

'What are the winters here like, anyway? I've only ever seen them through a window...' the owner of the tinkling voice said and Etta spied a blond girl of about her own age through Missus Mouse's window.

You're what...fifteen...sixteen...and you've never been allowed to go outside during winter?!?

The Mouse mumbled something unintelligible and said 'Harsh, the winters are harsh, girl, so pay attention and don't ruin any more of my stuff!'

'I will certainly try!' the girl said and nodded eagerly.

Was that coyness or sass or...was she being sincere?

The Mouse stomped off and Goldilocks as Etta dubbed her started singing.

Snow White's working song? Seriously?!?

Oooh-kay.

Etta retreated under a nearby tree and started chewing on a straw.

It was July.

The harsh winter the mouse had used to frighten the poor girl with was, in fact, far away.

There were no predators here, well, aside from whatever ate the bunny. She hadn't seen or heard anyone or anything since the bunny's unfortunate end, so Etta counted on living to see that harsh winter.

Which meant that at some point she, too, needed to start thinking about finding better lodgings than the hollow that had served her so well throughout the spring and summer.

Maybe the mouse could use another maid in exchange for room and board?

Except Etta would have to live with a fussy mouse and a Perky Patty.

All winter.

That would mean months of putting up with the both of them.

Etta sighed.

Maybe she'd take her chances in the woods after all.

Except nothing grew in the woods during winter and drinking only melted snow would not fill a stomach.

Etta sighed again.

It seemed that she didn't have much choice.

Needs must.

Fine!

But not before she got to know them both much better.

From afar.

Etta spent the best part of the day spying on the fairy who seemed to go about dusting and singing and trying really hard not to knock anything over.

The girl seemed honest and kind while the mouse seemed demanding. The girl didn't seem too put out no matter how the mouse addressed or treated her. She didn't even protest when the mouse locked her in and left.

Like she was happy no matter what.

All this scurrying and cleaning and the girl's wholesome goodness was giving Etta a headache.

If she was going to have a headache, she'd rather have it from trying to figure out how to penetrate that rubbery wall.

It was like a broken tooth, impossible to avoid, drawing her back despite the very real threat of ending up as someone's dinner.

Etta shook her head and prepared herself for the multi-day hike to the outskirts of her confined world when something flew through the air and hit her square in the head.

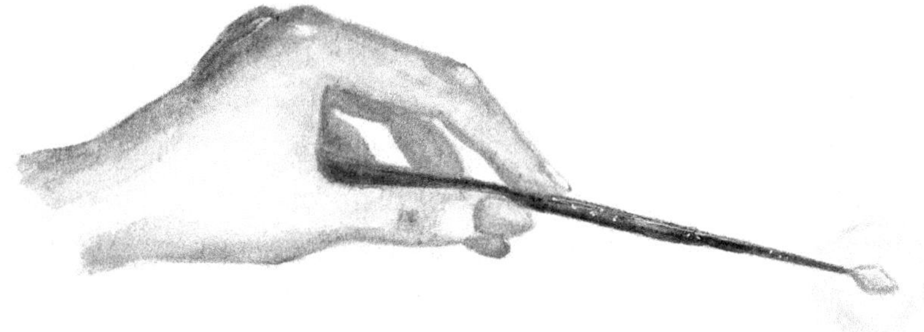

11. *'Blasted wand!'*

Chapter 16. Daisy

'Blasted wand!' yelled Missus Mouse's house guest.

Etta massaged her head and picked up the light-blue wand lying at her feet.

Before the girl could come out and retrieve the wand, Etta popped her head through the window and said, 'Lost something, did you?'

Goldilocks screamed and crouched behind a sturdy-looking armchair that took up most of the mouse's living room.

'Are you quite done?' Etta enquired. 'Screaming, I mean.'

'Why...y...yes,' the girl said from behind the chair.

'Then come on out, I'm the same size as you are, I couldn't possibly hurt you,' Etta said.

Having seen a few Jackie Chan movies, Etta had picked up a few moves, so that wasn't strictly true, but the fairy didn't need to know that.

'Goodness, I didn't realise someone else was here!' Goldilocks said, standing up and straightening her skirts. 'I thought the mouse and I were the only inhabitants of these woods,' she said.

'Yes, doesn't that seem strange to you that so very few creatures live here?' Etta asked and leaned on the window-sill.

Goldilocks looked worried, 'Be careful where you step, don't tread on my flowers, please!'

Etta glanced down.

Purple bellflowers with black shiny berries.

Belladonna.

'You obviously don't know much about flowers. These lovelies here are pure poison,' Etta said, 'Here, let me take care of it for you...so nobody gets hurt,' she raised her foot for a good stomp.

'Please don't! It's my only remedy against the mouse's constant vigilance!' Goldilocks pleaded.

Etta paused. 'Excuse me?'

'In very small doses, just a few *drops*[2], that plant is a sedative...and I need that sedative,' Goldilocks whispered. 'Just to rest... I'm not poisoning her or anything.'

Goldilocks wasn't as innocent as she looked. And the mouse seemed to be a handful.

Etta thought about it, finally nodded and hopped in through the window. 'Your secret is safe with me.'

Goldilocks exhaled in relief and plopped into the armchair.

'Yours?' Etta asked, handing back the wand.

The girl lit up for a second, remembered something and bit her lip. She inspected her wand. 'I don't know. I found it. But if it is mine, it is not very cooperative. It always switches off when I ask it to do menial work...' she mumbled, shook it and checked the batteries. 'Everything seems to be in order....'

'Try disenchanting it before you use it again,' Etta suggested.

The girl twirled her wand everywhichway, 'Are you sure it's enchanted? I mean, how can you tell?' she asked.

'Let's see. It only refuses to do one specific type of task?' Etta asked, picked up a blueberry from a fruit basket off the kitchen counter and bit into it as if it were an apple.

Goldilocks nodded.

'And you've had it for as long as you can remember?' Etta kept interrogating.

Goldilocks shook her head, 'No, it just appeared one day. With a note, saying to use it only in emergencies. And that day, boy was it an emergency! Missus Mouse had gone berserk again, there were scraps of food and fluff from her decorative pillows everywhere!! She hordes those pillows by the gazillion, you know...' she gushed as her visitor put up a hand.

'And did it?' Etta asked nodding at the wand, 'Clean?'

Daisy shook her head and bit her lip, 'Even though I keep trying,' she added. 'But in the end, I still have to do everything myself,' she sighed.

Etta looked around. Fruit baskets. Fresh linen. Everything not quite spotless but...clean.

Obviously, courtesy of the girl, not the mouse.

Clean but not quite clean...

Cleaning...

'Any chance menial tasks carry...a certain meaning for you?' Etta enquired between bites. 'So much so that you're willing to treat them as an emergency, which they aren't, you know...'

Goldilocks blushed, 'I really hate getting my hands dirty!' she burst out.

'Yeah, the place looks spotless,' *well, close enough,* 'because you hate cleaning...' Etta smirked and sent the berry skin flying out the window.

'Well, I hate squalor even more than cleaning and when enough gets to be enough...I clean,' the girl said and grimaced.

'And when you ask the wand to clean instead of you, it disobeys?' Etta asked, pretty sure she knew the answer.

Goldilocks sighed and nodded.

'En-chan-ted!' Etta sang. 'And by the looks of it, put there to test you.'

'Huh...' Goldilocks said and eyed her wand warily. 'If you know so much, how would you go about...disenchanting a wand?' she asked.

'What, no hello, how are you, who are you-s, straight to business?' Etta smirked.

'Oh, I do beg your pardon. Hello, how are you? I'm Daisy!' the blondie curtsied.

'Seriously? Did you just curtsy? To me?' Etta fell over laughing.

'I was just being careful. Ever heard of the Enchantress in the Beauty and the Beast? The prince was awful to her and she put an ugliness spell on him. I'd like to avoid that. I already have an enchanted wand to deal with,' Goldilocks said primly.

'Not only have I heard of that story, I know the Enchantress. Personally,' Etta sized up Daisy who looked suitably awed.

Well, she had met Caroline once, when the Fairy Queen had offered her that particular job.

'I'm Etta, by the way,' Etta said as the front door rattled.

'Now, where's that key?' they heard the mouse say.

'I'll get back to you about how to disenchant that wand,' Etta whispered and darted out the window and back into the ferns before Daisy could say 'thank you'.

12. *'Your secret is safe with me.'*

Chapter 17. Caroline

When Etta reached the wall, she heard sobbing.

It was faint and interrupted with hiccoughs, but it was definitely sobbing.

A loud wail pierced the air.

Someone was definitely crying their eyes out.

And it was most certainly a someone, because as far as Etta knew, mindless beasts who didn't speak also didn't cry.

She walked over to the wall and touched it.

Still solid.

Still rubbery.

But not soundproof.

Etta thought she saw the surface bulge towards her as if someone had leaned into the wall on the other side.

How was she going to get the attention of the person bawling on the other side?

Something flew through the air at Etta.

When she caught the thing, it turned out to be a wand.

There was a lot of that going around lately...

'Give it back, it's not yours!' said a rather familiar fairy, stepping through the wall.

Well, familiar without the wings she had somehow sprouted.

'Hello to you too, Caroline!' Etta said, 'I almost didn't recognise you.'

The girl she had watched rise from the dead was looking slightly wilted. Her parchment-like skin looked like it was one breeze away from disintegrating. Her wings looked brand new and magnificent. Etta thought she smelled funny, but didn't say anything.

'I know, don't I look amazing?' Caroline said, preening.

Etta rolled her eyes and mumbled, 'Maybe your mirror is enchanted...'

She handed Caroline her wand.

'You can pop over here,' Etta said, 'Can you pop back too?' she asked.

Let's hope she fares better than the hare. Etta hated experimenting on others, but aside from bumping against a rubbery surface, the hare hadn't come to any harm - well, at least not from the wall. Caroline should be fine. Besides, she was dead anyway, what could happen?

The winged fairy stepped across.

The wall let her pass without a glitch, parting to reveal a nocturnal forest on the other side.

'Why? Can't you?' Caroline asked over her shoulder as the invisible wall closed up behind her.

Etta shook her head, 'Nope.' She walked up to the barrier and pressed her palm against the rubbery wall. 'See, for me, there is a wall here while you can just walk through like it's air.'

'How very interesting,' Caroline said, stepping back to Etta's side, all uppishness gone from her voice. 'Why is that?'

Etta shrugged, 'No idea. I know that animals, too, can cross over here from the other side, but then they can't go back and then they...'

Get gobbled up?

'...they...'

End up as someone's snack?

'...disappear. And not in a nice way either.' Etta told Caroline and watched her blue eyes flash feral.

Maybe the red-rimmed glowing eye thing was the side-effect of being undead?

Maybe it was just a trick of the light?

'I remember the hare,' Caroline said, licking her lips, revealing small fangs Etta hadn't noticed the first time they had met.

Oooh-kay.

Not a trick of the light.

Well, now at least Etta knew what had happened to the hare.

Etta shrugged.

Some eat cooked vegetables, others don't. Some eat cooked meat, others love their boeuf a la tartar.

Out loud she said, 'My point was, I saw the hare try to get back to your side and it couldn't. Just like me. But you can. What makes you different?'

'I live on the other side?' Caroline offered.

'So did the hare,' Etta parried.

'I have wings...' Caroline said.

'Just now, you walked here and there, you didn't fly,' Etta said, eyeing the fairy carefully.

Caroline dangled her wand.

Etta squinted her eyes, 'I want to try something. May I?' she snatched the wand from Caroline and stuck it into the wall.

'Hey... wow, look at that, it goes through...' Caroline said.

'Yes, it does. Now, if I try to go with it...' Etta said as Caroline grabbed her by the hand.

'Oh, no you don't! Don't leave me here!' she pleaded.

Etta paused, 'Can we at least try to go through together?' she asked and Caroline nodded.

Etta took her by the sleeve, carefully avoiding contact with any decaying flesh and said, 'Lead on.'

They passed through the wall like a hot knife through butter.

The nocturnal forest swallowed the light and enveloped them in weird sounds and the same musky smell Etta had noticed emanating from Caroline.

Etta let go of Caroline's laced sleeve and blinked.

Maybe this entire forest smelled like decay, not just Caroline?

Etta froze.

Hearing the forest make so much noise at night was weird.

Amidst the see-saw of the crickets, she heard an owl hoot and the rustling wind up top made branches crack and trees groan.

Yep, definitely different from her enchanted nook of the forest.

Etta put her backhanded palm to this side of the wall.

Just as solid.

Just as rubbery.

The important question was - did the wall allow them through because of Caroline or because of her wand?

'Now that you're home safe, can I try this alone? Just once? Just to make sure? I will bring this back, I promise,' Etta said looking at the wand. When she looked at Caroline, her eyes were red-rimmed again and her fangs were protruding. Etta inhaled sharply.

I so hope she doesn't see me as the next bunny, Etta thought.

'What?' Caroline demanded.

'Nothing, absolutely nothing,' Etta mumbled. 'It's not like I can use it anyway, I don't know any spells. Right now, it's a means of transportation.'

She hoped.

'...And since I'm all alone on the other side...' Etta fibbed, 'Then I'd rather stay here and chat with you a bit longer, ok? I'll be back in a second, I promise,' she said and watched Caroline pout. But her eyes were dark blue again, and the fangs were gone.

Phew! Thank goodness, she could be normal when she wanted to.

As normal as one of the undead could be.

'Fine! But bring it back immediately!' the fairy ordered.

'Yes, m'am,' Etta said and dipped back through the wall to her side of the forest.

Daylight blinded her. Etta closed her eyes and turned her face up at the sun, feeling the fresh warm breeze.

She inhaled deeply.

Whaddaya know...it wasn't Caroline.

You had to have a wand to cross over.

Etta sighed and crossed back.

'You were gone a very long time!' Caroline complained.

'Yes, all of fifteen seconds,' Etta parried, 'Here you are, your wand.'

Caroline pocketed her prized possession. 'Follow me! You'll be my guest.'

Etta rolled her eyes. *The dead girl wasn't big on manners. Clearly, no thank-yous or pleases where she came from.*

But where exactly HAD she come from?

Before Etta could pry, Caroline said, 'I live over there!' she pointed towards a tiny cottage in the underbrush. 'Let's go have some tea!' Caroline took Etta by the sleeve and started pulling her towards her home.

Only the lonely, Etta thought and let herself be led.

Around them, the forest of firs swayed, chatted and lived.

***

After two pots of tea, curiosity got the best of Etta, 'Did she at least leave you a spell-book, like she promised?' Etta asked Caroline.

'Who left me what now?' Caroline asked and poured more tea.

'The Fairy Queen,' Etta said and Caroline bit her lip.

'Oh, I forgot, you were there, when she cursed me,' she said with a sour face, handing Etta her cup.

'Cursed you? The way I remember it, she tricked you with the lure of a prince and you were rather willing to go with her,' Etta said. 'Did you get your prince?'

'Does it look like I got my prince?' Caroline asked and gestured round her home.

'At least you live in a house, not in a tree hollow or under a fern,' Etta pointed out.

'Yes, I could be worse off,' Caroline said, picking at her lace sleeve.

Etta glanced at her.

Did she know?

Or was she completely oblivious that she was already off in the worst way imaginable?

Etta cleared her throat, 'So, about that spell-book the queen promised you....?'

'Book, what book?' Caroline widened her eyes. 'If you want a book, I have loads, pick one!' she gestured at walls of shelves laden with books.

When people widen their eyes, they are trying to look honest, which means they are lying their guts out, she remembered the old woman saying.

She couldn't help admiring the two solid walls of books.

How very Beauty and the Beast, indeed.

Since the direct approach did not work, it was time to use....what had the old woman called it? Reverse psychology or something like that.

Etta rolled her eyes, 'It figures, she lied about the prince as well as about the spell-book.'

Caroline shook her head, 'She didn't lie about the prince.'

'Ah-ha! Then she didn't lie about the book either!' Etta concluded and Caroline's parchment of a face vaguely changed colour.

'I bet you've tried to read the book and I bet it's in a language you don't know,' Etta continued.

Caroline glared at her, 'How dare you!'

'I bet you don't even know how to read!' Etta said and stuck out her tongue.

Caroline deflated mid-huff and sat down. 'How....how did you know?' she asked in a small voice.

What?

'What?' Etta said out loud.

'That I don't know how to read....' Caroline said and sniffled.

Oh no... She needed to do something to fix this. Before the waterworks started and Caroline's parchment-thin skin completely disintegrated.

Etta did the only thing she knew would work well as a distraction.

She volunteered.

'That's all right, I can help you read it, if you want....'

Caroline sniffled, 'I...I just thought I'd open the book and all the knowledge would somehow pour into me and I would just know how to do magic spells...' she sniffled again and wiped at her cheek, releasing a cloud of dust.

'I bet there's a spell in there that could magically make you understand any language, or at least human languages, but maybe also those of birds and bees and animals...' Etta knew she was rambling, but kept going seeing that Caroline's eyes had dried.

'You really think so? That I could learn the language of the birds and animals?' Caroline asked. 'I've always wanted to do that! Talk to animals...' she said wistfully and wandered over to the bookshelves.

Phew! Waterworks averted!

Caroline reached behind a hefty volume of a book Etta found familiar - *The Encyclopaedia of Plants and Herbs* - and tugged at something.

'Do you have any more tea?' Etta asked and headed for the kitchen, deciding to leave Caroline to her secret stashes.

When she returned with a steaming cup, Caroline was standing with her hands behind her back.

'What?' Etta put the cup down on the table and made herself comfortable in the armchair.

'Nothing,' Caroline said, smiling and dropped a leafy leather-bound volume into Etta's lap. ''Here! What does it say?'

Etta traced her finger across the leather cover.

'*Librum incantatorum* - the book of spells,' Etta translated and opened the book, 'Latin,' she said and her eyes lit up.

'You know the language?' Caroline was in awe. 'What does it say? Does it have any useful spells in it at all? Where's the spell about animal languages?' Caroline asked, standing behind Etta's armchair.

Etta squirmed. She had never been too fond of the old woman reading over her shoulder even when it was necessary. Like when she was teaching Etta to read.

Etta leafed through the tiny volume, 'Spell for forgetting things, spell for remembering things, spell for finding things...' *Nothing nasty.* 'It looks like these are all useful spells, as far as I can see...' Etta hoped there was a spell here on how to disenchant a wand. *Now that would be truly useful.*

'Well, at least she didn't lie about that,' Caroline said, perching herself on the arm of Etta's chair.

Etta closed the book.

Now that trust was established, there would be plenty of time to read the book later. First things first.

'What DID she lie about, Caroline? Tell me...please...' she asked quietly.

Caroline inclined her head, 'Well, not about the book and not about the wand and not about needing help.'

'Was there even a prince?' Etta asked when Caroline fell silent.

'There was, but like you had warned me, he wasn't meant for me. I was actually the one to turn him into a huge ugly beast, feared and loathed by all, including himself. I guess the name the queen wanted me to have - Enchantress - should have tipped me off. Now here I am, babysitting this boy of fifteen...' she sighed.

'What do you mean babysitting?' Etta asked.

'I have to turn him ugly every day so that the spell holds. Until someone - not me - comes along and falls in love with him just like he is, a beast. In one day! That's impossible!!! Let me tell you, anger on top of other teenage emotions is not particularly conducive to him being lovable. And he was mean to begin with,' Caroline complained.

'He was mean to you? Sounds like he deserved what he got,' Etta said.

'Not like this. Nobody deserves to be tortured for refusing to give food and shelter to a random filthy stranger. I mean, if someone you'd never met before who was ugly and in rags and muddy asked you to let them into your nice clean home, would you have let them? I know I wouldn't have, that's for sure.' Caroline said. 'Even for a fifteen-year-old, that was sound judgement, I think, but what I think doesn't count. I still have to enchant him every day even though he has begged me not to. Oh, how he has begged...' Caroline sighed.

'So, he said he was sorry and you think he was right for not helping a muddy stranger and still you have to be the bad guy?' Etta asked and Caroline nodded. 'That's...not fair,' Etta said and Caroline nodded again. 'Have you tried NOT enchanting him?' Etta asked.

Caroline nodded again and sniffled, 'The next day I'm the one who wakes up as the Beast. I get to be the Beast for one day while he is stuck being some inanimate object I cannot even find in his castle! The morning after I wake up as me and he wakes up as himself and we have to go through with it all over again. Unless I want to be the Beast for another day.'

Etta had no comeback about such cruelty.

An uneasy silence fell.

'Looks like your fairy godmother, was not very honest with you...' Etta finally summed up.

'Oh, she's no godmother at all. At least I don't think that's how godmothers are supposed to behave, you know,' Caroline sniffled.

Before the waterworks started again, Etta opened the book, 'Shall we have a look for that animal language spell, what do you think?'

'Ooh, yes, please!' Caroline said and plopped into the chair next to Etta's, folding her wings on the go.

The dust and odour that billowed made Etta almost gag, but she kept her cool. 'Now, let's see...'

Two intensive hours later, Etta couldn't keep her eyes open anymore. Also, all the excitement had made Caroline smell even worse, if that was possible. 'As exciting as learning various animal languages and learning how to read and turning every inanimate object you have here into animate and back is, I'm done for tonight,' Etta yawned, rose and threw open the window. Much welcome fresh air whooshed in together with an owl hoot.

Etta hadn't noticed a disenchantment spell, but tomorrow was another day.

'Oh, I don't need any sleep, we can go on and on...' Caroline said, eyes ablaze.

'You do that. I need sleep,' Etta said and curled up under a throw in Caroline's armchair. 'Just don't turn me into anything nasty,' Etta managed to mumble, falling asleep as soon as her head hit the armrest.

Chapter 18. Gifts With Strings

When Etta returned to Missus Mouse's cottage hoping to catch Daisy, she found the door ajar.

The lights were out.

Etta knocked.

No one answered.

The fairy went in and looked around.

The house looked like a dump.

There were scraps of food on the floor, used cups and plates stacked up on the window-sill, throws hanging from the lamp, walls covered with goose-feathers.

Fluff from pillows.

Missus Mouse's decorative pillows.

Well, by the looks of it, Missus Mouse had gone berserk again.

Where was Daisy?

Etta surveyed the carnage.

If she had to clean it up, she'd quit and run away too.

The only clean space in the entire room was a small coffee table next to the fireplace, sporting a piece of parchment next to a light-blue wand.

Daisy's wand.

Etta doubted any fairy would leave their wand behind.

Something wasn't right.

'My dear, keep this gift safe and do use it only in emergencies!' was all the note said.

Apparently, whoever the well-wisher was, they had counted on the next fairy coming along...

'Why is my home still messy? I leave you alone for a couple of hours and you cannot manage to clean it up, girl? I think we need to revisit our room and board agreement,' Missus Mouse said from behind Etta.

Apparently, all fairies looked the same to Missus Mouse.

'Yes, we really do need to revisit our agreement. If you're going to keep doing this,' Etta gestured at the room.

'What? Are you talking back to me, Daisy?' the mouse wriggled her whiskers.

'Look, Missus. I'm not Daisy,' Etta said, pocketing the wand.

'Oh...oh...' the mouse adjusted her glasses and blinked myopically. 'No, I guess you're not. If you're not Daisy, who are you, dear?' she asked, fidgeting.

'I'm Etta. And I guess you need someone to clean and maybe cook?' she asked as the mouse nodded quickly.

Summer was fun in the forest. But autumn was nigh and so was winter and she needed a warmer place to spend winter than in a tree hollow.

Etta continued, 'Well, you're in luck. I cook. As about cleaning, I dust and vacuum alright, but we'll have to do something about your temper tantrums. Why'd you have those anyway?' she asked and handed the shocked mouse a throw she took down from the ceiling lamp.

The mouse blinked and wriggled her whiskers, but started to fold the throw anyway.

***

During the entire month of August Etta tried to get used to living in closed surroundings with a twitchy room-mate. The mouse had a bad habit of sticking her nose everywhere, ordering Etta around and getting in her way. That's when she wasn't going berserk, which was at least once a week.

The mouse was nosey AND controlling.

'Girl, do this!' and 'Girl, fetch that!' and 'Girl, get away from that door!'

As if she wanted to see the mouse's secret stash of a pantry.

All women are allowed their secrets, she remembered the old woman saying.

Why would she bother with some stupid door when she had the forest to escape to!

Whenever her chores were done, Etta slipped out to get some space. Even if this forest was enchanted, room to roam was what she craved.

She even ventured back to the wall, but couldn't figure out how to get to Caroline on the other side.

That next morning, they had overslept and Caroline had been in such a hurry to get to the Beast that they had forgotten to agree on how to keep in touch or signal each other. Nor did Etta get another peek at the spell-book.

So much for the disenchantment spell.

She had realised their mistake as soon as she had groggily stumbled through the wall and seen Caroline disappear behind the partition, taking her wand with her.

You would think Caroline would come looking for her.
Nope.

She hadn't seen the other fairy in a month.

Etta was starting to think Caroline's no-show was not accidental.

If I wouldn't see her for a month and I knew that she can't cross over to my side, I would go looking for her.
Why didn't SHE?
The again, why would she?
Caroline had her freedom, she as probably having fun with her wand and spells.

Etta had made the mistake of forgetting how self-involved Caroline was.

Another mistake was not making time to get the spell she needed.

She had tried Daisy's wand - well, *her* wand now - to cross over, only to bump her nose against the rubbery surface that refused to budge.

It seemed that her wand was a limited edition for doing limited things. It was useless for crossing purposes. It was useless for cleaning.

In fact, Etta hadn't had the opportunity to use it for anything much.

There was no point in trying the animal language spell since the mouse spoke English.

Otherwise, it was just a shiny blue stick.

Rather good for getting down the cobwebs from the ceiling, though.

Either it was Caroline's wand that she needed or she needed to disenchant Daisy's wand first.

The wand fiasco or her doubts hadn't stopped her from camping out at the wall whenever she could get away from the mouse.

Like today.

Etta got up from the grass and patted her apron pocket. She had made a note about all the spells she needed for the next time she crossed over.

If there ever was a next time.

Etta put her hand out and touched a familiar rubbery surface.

The wall was still there.

Check.

She put her ear to the wall.

No sound and no movement on the other side.

Check.

She yelled, 'Caroline! I'm here, come get me!'

The cottage was at a distance, but maybe Caroline would be walking by, trying to find her as well?

No answer.

Check.

Etta tried sticking her wand into the wall and it bounced off.

Same as last time.

Check.

Etta kicked at the wall.

There was nothing else she could do.

Except come back another time and hope for the better.

Etta took one last look.

No change.

Check.

She had given it a fair try.

Again.

Etta sighed.

Time to go back to the house the mouse had built.

She was sure the mouse would have things to say about her two-day absence.

Then, again, maybe not.

The mouse occasionally left for days and refused to talk about her absences, pretending as if they hadn't happened.

That and her hostess' lapses in memory were a bit worrisome.

Etta had tried prying into what had happened to Daisy, but the mouse had feigned ignorance that there had ever been another fairy in the house and nearly called Etta a liar.

Alzheimer's, as the old woman would say.

Etta sighed and turned to go back to slavery via the graveyard slash hatching site.

13. *Why is my home still messy?'*

Chapter 19. Annabel's Baby

Approaching the graveyard, Etta noticed a pair of familiar blue wings seated on the bark of the maple.

Could it be?

'Annabel?' she asked.

The butterfly eyed her coldly.

'It is you, isn't it?' Etta said.

The butterfly continued ignoring her.

'Listen, I'm so sorry that I didn't untie you. I really am! The bug carried me off and I didn't know it was going to just fly away and it refused to go back and then it turned out...' Etta gushed.

'If you want to apologise, you shouldn't spew excuses,' Annabel said curtly.

'Quite right. And I can see you're still mad at me. I was so relieved when I heard that you'd gotten away...' Etta said.

'No thanks to you,' the butterfly huffed.

'And congratulations on the marriage! And becoming the president of the Veteran's club? Wow!' Etta said and thought *how do you hug an angry butterfly?*

'Thank you,' Annabel said and looked up, 'Look, it's hatching!'

'Your baby?' Etta asked. 'Is he? She? A *Heliconius* as well?' she asked.

Annabel hunhed, 'Do you think I'd wed a moth or something?' she asked. 'Of course, my baby is a *Heliconius*! Oh, no. Not yet. It was just a falling leaf.'

The yellow maple leaf tinged with maroon at the edges wafted down and Etta had to duck so as not to get flattened.

So, that's why the Americans call it the Fall, instead of autumn.

Out loud Etta said, 'In any case, congratulations! I'm so happy for you!'

'Thank you,' Annabel said, slightly mollified.

After a long silence - Etta really didn't know what else to say - the butterfly couldn't help herself, 'Do YOU have anyone special in your life to make babies with?'

Etta shook her head no. She had only seen male fairies in the story-books the old woman had shown her. She knew they existed, she just hadn't met any.

Annabel hunhed.

'What, you don't think I'll find anyone?' Etta asked.

As true as that may be in this neck of the woods, she couldn't believe she was getting comments about her love life from an insect.

'You are far too careless,' the butterfly said, 'And fickle.'

Etta was tempted to tell Annabel that she was basing her judgement on half a day that they spent together four months ago, but bit her tongue.

Plenty had happened in four months and she was glad to talk to someone other than the mouse.

She didn't want to upset Annabel again, in the hope that the butterfly could either help her get away or at least be a source of information.

'Building relationships takes time and patience, you know.' Annabel said. 'It took my husband one week to woo me.'

Etta did a quick calculation.

One week out of six months that the Heliconii lived was 1/24 of their lifetime. For humans with an average life span of eighty years, that would be... three years and four months of wooing.

For fairies, who knew what was appropriate?

Etta didn't know how long fairies lived. The old woman had never shared that knowledge, perhaps because she didn't know herself.

'So, what you're saying is that you don't believe I will ever find a mate...' Etta asked. *When others tell you things you don't want to hear, try to clarify what they mean or agree with the least possible bit of information that you can agree with,* she remembered the old woman saying.

'I didn't say never,' Annabel said, 'but probably not until you grow up,' the butterfly said.

'I'm almost sixteen. I'm all grown up,' Etta said, confident this was true.

'You're such a baby! The confidence of youth,' Annabel hunhed.

'Are you saying babies always think they are very mature?' Etta asked.

Annabel threw her a glance and didn't answer.

Uh-oh, Etta needed to keep the conversation going, if she ever wanted to get out of here.

'Ok, ok, if I'm immature, what if my future mate is as immature as I am?' Etta asked and muttered, 'According to you anyway...' *There were worse things than immature. Like mean.*

'Then bless you both, for you would deserve each other,' the butterfly said and meant it.

'About finding me that someone special... There are no fairy men in this neck of the woods...would you be so kind and...' Etta started.

'No!' Annabel fluttered her wings. 'No ferrying you anywhere. How can you even ask me that after what you did? Don't you see I have a new addition to my family on the way?' she nodded up at the cocoon. 'I have a family I need to take care of. Have you ever considered what would happen to my babies?'

Etta bit her lip.

She hadn't.

She had just relied on the belief that Annabel was programmed to help fairies.

'No, of course you haven't thought about anything but yourself! Your selfishness astounds me! And proves, once again, that you really are immature!'

Ok, if she had to resort to only herself to get out of this enchanted place, then some information would be helpful.

But she'd let Annabel calm down first.

'I'm sorry,' Etta said.

Annabel nodded, accepting the apology.

They were silent for a while.

'If there are no fairy men here to make babies with, why are you here?' Annabel asked.

Etta exhaled, 'I found out I couldn't leave these woods. There is only this mouse, nobody else,' Etta remembered the May bugs, 'Well, nobody I care to talk to and I cannot get to another friend of mine and a girl has gone missing...'

Annabel fluttered her wings, 'No, I mean, why are you here here?'

'You mean at this graveyard?' Etta asked.

'Hatching site,' Annabel corrected her.

'Hatching site, beg your pardon!' Etta parroted.

'Yes. Why are you here now?' Annabel asked.

'Well, I found this place by accident...and met a butterfly who told me that she knows you and you were just married... and after I'd given all the dead butterflies a proper send-off I figured I'd come and wait for you...' Etta said and added 'For as long as it took...' *Which was four months.*

Annabel wriggled her feelers, 'You waited here...for me? Why?'

'To apologise for leaving you tied up and helpless,' Etta said. 'I'm sorry.'

'I'm not helpless. I was never helpless. I could get help and I did get help, knowing the usual fate that befell a butterfly who helped a fairy...' Annabel snapped.

'Oh...great! That is so great that you thought ahead! I have so much to learn from you...' Etta said. *Within the next few weeks or however long Annabel had left.*

Annabel fluttered her wings, 'Well, perhaps you do...'

Flattery will get you anywhere, as the old woman used to say.

'In the spirit of learning...Annabel, are butterflies special?' Etta asked.

'Special? Of course, we are, every single one of us. Why do you ask?'

'Well, you can come to this river nook...to your hatching site...and go from here, as you please...' Etta mused.

'Yes, we can fly in anytime,' Annabel confirmed.

'Fly...you fly...and when you fly, you are not restricted in your movements in any way?' Etta asked.

'Restricted how?' Annabel asked, looking up and sighing.

'Oh, I don't know...is there any part near the river or in the forest where you cannot fly?' Etta asked.

'What do you mean? I CAN fly anywhere,' Annabel said.

'Yes, but DO you fly everywhere or is there a place that you try to avoid or...were told to avoid, maybe?' Etta asked. 'You didn't want to fly south with me...'

Annabel fell silent. 'You're talking about the cursed place,' she whispered.

'The cursed place, which cursed place?' Etta whispered back.

'You know which one, otherwise you wouldn't have asked,' Annabel said.

'So, you avoid it,' Etta said.

'We avoid it,' Annabel said.

'But...could you....fly over it, if you wanted to? I mean, has anyone ever tried?' Etta asked.

Annabel looked at her reproachfully, 'Of course, we can fly over it, but we don't. It's part of the deal...'

'What deal is that? Part of the deal to ferry fairies wherever they need to be ferried?' Etta asked.

Annabel nodded and kept schtum.

Was there a vertical boundary to the 'cursed place' as Annabel had put it? Or did it prevent everybody who wasn't a butterfly or didn't have a wand who got in from ever getting out again? The bunny was bound to the ground, as was Etta. May bugs weren't.

'Annabel, have any of the butterflies gone missing when they have flown over the 'cursed place'?' Etta asked.

Annabel looked at her reproachfully, 'Are you dumb or something?'

Etta blinked back the insult.

'How would I know which ones have gone missing because they ferried fairies compared with those that have gone missing because they flew over the cursed place?' the butterfly scoffed.

True.

A thought occurred to Etta.

'But you can come and go here, to this...erm...hatching site. Across the river...and back...and forth...' Etta mused.

'And back and forth, yes, what's your point?' the butterfly asked and looked up again.

The point was, the river was wide open.

Of course, there was no need to put a protective wall up there.

Who would be crazy enough to try and escape via the river?

Not wingless fairies, surely.

It wasn't because the butterflies were special that there was no enchanted wall at the riverbank.

It was because no wingless fairy had tried escaping that way.

Except she had to find a way that didn't involve Annabel.

First, because Annabel had turned her down flat.

Second, because it wasn't fair to ask for Annabel's help, when she only had a few weeks to live and raise her last kid. Six months was a short life-span and Annabel's six months were almost up.

And third, because she didn't know what instructions Annabel had in the event a fairy from the cursed place made the butterfly take her across the water. For sure, Annabel knew more than she was letting on. Who knew, maybe she was told to 'accidentally' drop such a fairy to her death when trying to help her escape the enchanted woods?

After all, May bugs goaded Caroline to jump.

Who's to say that butterflies didn't have similar orders?
Etta wasn't taking any chances.
She was done relying on others to escape.
Out loud, Etta said, 'No point, really.'

Annabel glanced up and emitted a high-pitched squeal, all of Etta's nosiness forgotten.

'Now she's really hatching!' Annabel fluttered her wings. 'Look, look!'

'How do you know it's a she?' Etta wondered out loud, craning her neck to see.

'A mother just knows,' Annabel said and went to help her kid.

14.   *'Now she's really hatching!'*

Chapter 20. The Mole

Etta had been an unpaid live-in maid for two months when at the first sight of snow, the mouse told her to bake her a cake.

'A cake? Why? I've never noticed that you have a sweet tooth.' Etta said, secretly glad she had observed the old woman make cakes countless of times.

The mouse snickered, nodded and scurried off.

Probably to replenish her supplies before winter finally hit.

Etta was decorating her cake with blueberries when she heard a key being turned in a lock. When she peeked into the living room, she saw the hidden door to the pantry slowly opening. The same door that the mouse had forbidden her to open. The one she claimed led to her winter stash of their food.

By the looks of it, their winter stash was attempting a prison break.

Etta wiped her hands into her apron and took the huge stick Missus Mouse occasionally made her use to beat the dust out of the rugs.

The door creaked open and darkness spilled into the living room.

Etta raised the stick, ready to swing and observed the darkness spilling further and further until it reached the mouse's favourite armchair and sat itself down in the form of a mole. The armchair's legs squeaked as it sagged under his weight.

'Who the hell are you? You shouldn't sneak up on people! I almost clubbed you!' Etta yelled and the entire armchair jumped.

'Erm...hello? I didn't know anyone was home...' the creature stuttered.

'So you're in the habit of popping by when nobody's home, are you? Should we hide our valuables now or wait until you leave?' Etta asked, knowing how ridiculous she sounded. *The dude was blind!*

The mole huffed, 'Well I never...'

'And what about the paw marks?' Etta asked, pointing at the muddy trail from the door to the chair.

'Missus Mouse usually has a girl for that...' the mole waved her off.

'Well, I'm the girl and I won't stand for it! I just cleaned those floors an hour ago! I'm not going to do it again!' Etta snapped.

'Oh, yes you are,' said Missus Mouse to her and 'Hello, Mister Mole! So nice of you to visit us!' to her guest.

'I didn't know there was an 'us', otherwise...otherwise I'd have brought gifts...' the mole sputtered, wriggling his whiskers.

Etta didn't understand what did the number of people you were going to visit have to do with the common courtesy of never visiting empty-handed. Noticing the paw marks again she rolled her eyes. 'Wipe your feet the next time, will you!' the fairy ordered, 'the door mat has a function, you know! In fact, I'm going to put another one outside that door.'

'Which one of them do you want me to use, then?' The mole asked.

'How about both of them?' Etta suggested.

'Stop your bickering! Now, girl, go make us some tea!' the mouse ordered.

'I'll make you a deal, I'll go make your tea, if you clean those up,' she said, her hands on hips.

'Oh, pish-posh... Tea! Now!' The mouse said.

Etta rolled her eyes once more and went to fetch their tea.

When she returned ten minutes later, the paw marks were still there.

Etta set the tea-pot down and asked, 'Shall I go fetch the mop for you?'

Missus Mouse glanced at her, 'What? Now? Sure, if you like...'

When Etta returned and handed her the mop. The mouse looked at it like she was seeing it for the first time. It occurred to Etta that she probably was.

'What's this?' The mouse asked.

'This is a mop,' Etta said.

Mop, meet mouse, mouse, meet mop.

'What am I to do with it?' The mouse looked puzzled.

'Well, you can wet it and then scrub that mud or you can wait 'till it dries a bit and then wipe it,' Etta offered helpfully.

'Oh, I'm doing no such thing, that's what I have you for,' the mouse giggled and returned to her conversation about building better tunnels.

Etta bit her lip, nodded and went to the kitchen grabbing the tea-pot on the fly.

If she was the cleaner, she was going to clean. It wasn't her problem that they weren't done with their tea yet!

Etta muttered and clanged the bucket at anything and everything as she scrubbed the drying mud off the floor.

When she was done, Missus Mouse handed her the empty cups and said, not unkindly, 'You didn't have to do that now, you know?'

A moment later Etta realised why.

The mole stood up to leave and shuffled back to the door, leaving dirt in his wake.

Of course, she'd forgotten that he hadn't washed his paws! She'd have to do it all over again!

She growled so loudly she made them both jump.

'Use. The. Mat. Next. Time. Both. Of. Them!' She said through gritted teeth and stomped off.

She'd have to figure out how to secure the door so as to prevent the critter from entering at all hours of day and night. Until he learnt to wipe his feet anyway.

Doubting this would be his only visit, she'd also have to figure out how to survive this long winter with such annoying guests dropping in.

Chapter 21. Tall Orders

Missus Mouse was looking tipsy, courtesy of Etta dosing her with a few drops of the deadly nightshade.

Well, courtesy of Daisy, actually, who had pointed out the belladonna growing under the mouse's window. Etta had just had the good sense to dig up the flowers, put them in a pot and the pot into the corner behind the stove when the first snow arrived. She had distilled a bottle of drops from the rest of her harvest, hoping the quantity would last until spring.

If she stayed here that long.

She had counted out two drops for the huge pot of tea she had made.

Now, all she had to do was wait.

A lightweight like the mouse should nod off in no time.

Then she could put her to bed and go check on the wall in the hope of seeing Caroline.

'Sing for me,' the mouse said and when Etta stared at her, added with bravado, 'Or we could sing together!'

As if. Two pipsqueaks not a merry tune make.

'That's a tall order. Work AND sing? What am I, Snow White? What makes you think I can?' Etta asked.

'I've heard you hum when you do your chores,' the mouse said sneakily. 'You can carry a tune, I know you can.'

'Ok, I'll sing and then you'll do the dishes, how about it?' Etta tried to bargain.

The mouse waved a paw at her and poured herself some more tea. 'Fui! If you won't do the dishes, I assume you don't want to eat?'

'I'm the one doing the cooking. You'd have to stand real close to try and stop me and then I might get careless with the knife and chop something of yours off...' Etta said almost absent-mindedly.

Missus Mouse chortled, 'That's funny...'

Etta raised an eyebrow.

She hadn't meant to be funny.

She had meant for the mouse to get the point - that she needed to start pitching in.

Etta had too much to do and too little time to explore. She had discovered that compared to the freedom she had enjoyed in the summer, restricted movement was not her thing.

How she had managed to be happy being confined to just one room and on occasion to just one plate at the old woman's place, was beyond improbable now.

She needed some rest!

Etta would have loved nothing more than dose the mouse's tea with more belladonna, except she didn't want the mouse to overdose. A few drops too many and the sleep would be the Big Slumber.

'Even if you chopped off some bits...the bits that you could take...you cannot take anything from me that actually matters...,' the mouse snickered.

Whoa, that was way too deep, even for a tipsy mouse.

'I was married once, you know...' the mouse said, settling herself into the armchair. 'Wedded by THE Fairy Queen, I'll have you know,..lovely ceremony, just lovely...,' the mouse closed her eyes, reminiscing.

The Fairy Queen?

Could it be the same one that had whisked Caroline away?

Since it was so unlike the Missus to volunteer any information, Etta pretended to do the dusting as if she wasn't listening, but perked up her ears.

'Mister Mouse was wonderful. Simply wonderful. I mean I only met him one day, married him the next and all we had was our wedding night, but still... it was all...simply wonderful...' the mouse was nearly nodding off.

'What happened to him? Why did he leave?' Etta asked, not being able to help herself.

'Oh, he didn't go. He was taken from me,' the mouse said sadly and got up to pour herself a drop more.

'Taken?' Etta whispered, shuddering. 'By whom?' Etta doubted toads ventured this deep into the forest.

'I don't know by whom,' the Missus said and sighed, her button eyes misting over. 'On the morning after our wedding I woke up and he was gone. His toothbrush was there, his slippers, even the tea was still steaming in his mug on the kitchen counter. The door was wide open and the rug was upturned, there was a torn piece of cloth on the nail next to the door where the keys go... He couldn't, he just couldn't have left in such a hurry as not to even leave me a note about why or where he had to go or when he would be back! He was taken from me!' the mouse said with conviction. 'Married one day, widowed the next...' the mouse mumbled.

Having heard rather awkward stories from the old woman about husbands stepping out for a pint of milk or cigarettes and never coming back, Etta was sceptical.

'The woods...they used to be so alive, you know?' the mouse said wistfully as Etta held her breath. 'My husband, he was the first to be taken...then it was the neighbours, then the hedgehogs who used to scurry around delivering everybody's messages, then one day there were no more animals in the underbrush. No more birds of prey either and that was a bit alarming at first... Then, thankfully I discovered Mister Mole was also spared and I was relieved...' the mouse started nodding off in her armchair.

Spared? By whom?

So it wasn't a coincidence that Etta couldn't find any animals in this neck of the woods, on this side of the invisible wall.

'At least we had our wedding night,' Missus Mouse stirred, 'and if it hadn't been for the constant worry over what happened to him...if it hadn't been for that, I might not be alone right now...' she said very very quietly.

'You had a baby?' Etta asked carefully, not sure she had understood the mouse correctly.

'Almost...I almost had many, many babies,' the mouse whispered, her eyes drifting shut, 'if the vigour of Mister Mouse on our wedding night was anything to go by, we should have had many, many, many babies...and often... alas, it was not meant to be...I lost them, too...' she said, 'and when I remember how much I have lost, I sometimes lose myself too, you know....' Her head dipped.

That's why the mouse sometimes went berserk?

'Sing something for me, will ya?' Missus Mouse asked as she jerked her head up and Etta didn't have the heart to refuse.

Miscarriage on top of losing a loved one was, after all, a terrible thing.

***

When the mouse was sound asleep, Etta laid the lady into her cot and covered her up.

Standing above the tiny critter, Etta contemplated all she had learnt.

If Mister Mouse was taken, it begged two questions: by whom and why?

It was as if this area was specifically created, walled off and cleared...

The mouse snorted in her sleep.

...Well, nearly cleared from fauna for some specific reason.

What did the May bugs, the mouse and the mole have in common?

Etta couldn't see the answer.

Maybe she was looking at this wrong.

Why were the bugs, the mole and the mouse spared while everyone else was wiped out?

Caroline had also met the May bugs.

Daisy and Etta both knew the mouse.

Etta never got to ask, but maybe Daisy also knew the bugs and the mole?

Maybe whatever was going on here had something to do with fairies and the scary Fairy Queen who could raise the dead?

She had brought Caroline back to life.

Perhaps, she had also wed the mice.

She definitely had some deal going on with the May bugs.

Etta wished she could talk to Caroline and Daisy. Three heads were better than one for figuring this puzzle out.

She had no way of reaching them, much less getting them together in one space at the same time.

Out of sheer doggedness she decided she should brave a trek to the wall and try to break through to Caroline.

Except now with the snow, she had to take supplies and something warm to wear plus pick a sunny day so she could make an occasional fire by using the shard of glass she had set aside when the mouse had broken a mirror.

Fire!

Maybe Caroline would notice the fire on the other side and come looking for her!

Right.

Before her trek, she should pack up, take one of the mouse's woollen throws with her and...take care of other, more pressing matters.

Etta grabbed the woollen throw and went out the door.

Just as she was sitting down in the bushes for a restful pee she found herself in the middle of Caroline's living room.

'Oi, not on my rug!' Caroline yelled and all of Etta's basic needs were forgotten.

Etta quickly straightened her skirts and managed to ask 'Peep much?' before Caroline disappeared.

Right.

Well, at least Caroline was trying to figure out how to get in touch.

In a considerably better mood, Etta ventured back to retrieve her supplies.

Caroline hadn't given up on her.

That was the good news.

The bad news was, whatever she had tried, hadn't worked.

Maybe now Caroline would have the good sense to go to the wall to wait for her?

Before she headed out, Etta looked in on the mouse one last time.

One of the mouse's stockinged paws had escaped from under the duvet.

Etta carefully stuck it back and got a snort in return as gratitude.

The critter looked so tiny and pathetic in her cap and her striped stockings, huddled in a bunch under the huge duvet.

If she were to leave now...tonight...

There was nobody to take care of this pathetic creature and if she lost one more thing in her life, who knew what she would do.

Etta sighed and dropped her satchel with a small kathunk.

The mouse snorted again, but didn't wake.

Who knew, maybe she'd given her too much belladonna.

She needed to stay and make sure the mouse woke up.

What's another day to the undead?

Caroline could wait.

So could Etta's questions and her trek.

Chapter 22. The Worms

The next morning, Etta heard knocking. The hollow sound reverberated through the entire house. It reminded Etta of drumming on the old empty wine barrels in the old woman's garden.

When she was still allowed into the garden.

When she still lived with the old woman, which seemed to be several lifetimes ago.

Etta eyed the back door and prayed it wasn't who she thought it was.

'Hello?' The mole said hesitantly. 'Anyone home?'

'Hello!' Etta rolled her eyes and said, 'I'll go fetch Missus Mouse for you.'

'Oh, no, not just yet. Here,' the critter thrust something at her.

When Etta realised what it was, she almost dropped the can.

Worms.

Wriggling worms.

Eeeuw!

'Are you going fishing later?' Etta enquired.

Maybe he didn't know it was winter outside and that all nature was frozen?

Maybe he was into ice fishing

'I'll put those into storage for you...' Etta said.

Ice cold storage.

Outside.

In the snow.

The mole looked confused.

'Missus Mouse!' Etta yelled.

'No need to yell, dear, I'm right here,' the mouse said, straightening her cap and apron.

If that was her attempt at flirting, Etta was tempted to remind her that her beau was blind.

'If you are right here, then you can tend to your guest,' Etta said instead.

'*Our* guest and go make us some tea!' The mouse ordered.

'May I remind you that I'm not your servant, but a paying guest?' Etta told her.

'Paying in kind and the kind I'm talking about makes tea for me and my guests,' the mouse snapped.

Etta went to the kitchen and took down the cups from the top cupboard only to find the mouse staring at her crossly.

'Be nice to my guests,' the mouse said and tap-tapped her foot.

'Guests as in plural? How many more are coming?' Etta specified.

'Just Mister Mole, but you get my point!' The mouse said and Etta nodded.

'What is this?' The Missus pointed at the dirty can Etta had covered with a saucer to prevent the worms from escaping.

'Mister Mole's worms. I think he brought you a gift or else he's going ice fishing later,' Etta said.

'Me? No-no, if he gave them to you, it's your gift, dear,' the mouse said tartly. 'And don't cover them up with my good saucers!' She hissed.

'Right, I'll go throw them out then,' Etta said.

'You'll do no such thing! It's a gift!!' The mouse hissed again.

'If it's my gift, then I can do whatever I want with it. If he wanted to bring me a gift, someone' Etta made a face, 'might clue him up that flowers are a way better gift anytime.'

'What flowers? It's winter!! Besides, Mister Mole never goes up top!' The mouse hissed again. 'And he hates flowers!'

'With gifts it is customary to give the other person what they like and not what the giver likes or so I'm told,' Etta stage-whispered. 'In any case - anything would be better than worms!' Etta hissed.

Chapter 23. Incredibly Untrue

The next evening Etta got a flower drawn in crayon on toilet paper.

Be careful what you wish for, she muttered. *My-my, the mole had keen hearing or they hadn't been whispering quietly enough yesterday.*

A drawing by the blind was tremendous effort, she had to give him that.

Unless the mouse had helped.

Still, no amount of flowers on toilet paper was going to make up for Etta's daily cleaning of muddy paw marks off the floor.

Hearing the mole droning on and on about one complaint or another in the next room, Etta thought *And no paper flowers were going to make up for having to listen to you either.*

'Last winter, when I happened to go up top, I was almost blinded by the sun, you know,' the mole said to Missus Mouse who clucked her discontent.

If you had worn your sunglasses like normal beings when it is sunny and there is snow, you wouldn't have to complain, Etta thought.

'The sun is the most wretched thing up top, I tell you. Even though I am challenged in the sight department, it physically hurts my eyes, when the damn things shines straight into them. I can feel its penetrating stare!'

Then you shouldn't look straight into it, you fool, Etta thought. *It's not like the sun can look away.*

'We could do without it, I reckon. The sun, I mean. At least we would if it was up to me,' he added and smacked his lips, chewing open-mouthed on the blueberry pie Etta had made.

His favourite.

I'm so glad it's not up to you, Etta thought.

'Awful, simply awful,' the mouse said and asked, 'Would you like some more tea, Mister Mole?'

When she received a curt nod from her gentleman caller, she ordered, 'Girl, make us some more tea!'

Etta sighed and put away the mop she had grabbed to swipe the mole's muddy paw marks.

If she didn't clean them now, the both of them would traipse through the trail and drag it across all of the house and then she'd have to do a spring clean in the middle of winter.

'Tea? What kind of tea?' she asked.

Missus Mouse looked at her reproachfully, 'Whatever is in the cupboard, dear.'

'There is lots, which is why I'm asking. Camomile or dandelion or maple leaves or elder-flowers or peppermint or...' she began listing.

'Not dandelion! Nothing from the flowers! I hate the wretched things!' the mole protested.

'Are trees alright or do you hate them too?' Etta asked, putting the kettle on.

'Don't be daft, make it peppermint, as always,' the mouse ordered, 'And bring us the porcelain cups, not like the last time,' she hissed.

'It's not like he can see to appreciate them,' Etta mumbled, wondering why the mouse was so hospitable all of a sudden when her, now daily, visitor was nothing short of appalling.

I guess loneliness has its price.

Before the mole could launch into yet another complaint about some thing or another, the mouse said, 'You know, the girl was telling me the funniest story this morning, something about butterflies and gambling, completely made up, of course, oh, I don't remember it all precisely... Tell the story again, girl!' she ordered.

'I have a name. It's Etta, not girl and like I told you yesterday, when I told you the story, it isn't made up, it's all true and not funny at all,' Etta said, bringing them their tea.

She had told the mouse about the butterflies partly because she thought one of the three ground inhabitants of this part of the woods might as well know SOMETHING about the world out there, partly to distract the mouse from her dark thoughts and partly because she wanted to know if the mouse knew more than she let on. While her hostess had certainly brightened at the tale, she had parted with no extra information.

Etta's questions were still questions.

'Your favourite cups,' she said, setting them on the table.

'What did you do that for?' the mouse hissed, 'my second best would have been just as nice,' she whispered eyeing the movements of her guest very closely.

Yes, now you'll have to watch the mole every second and pray that your favourite cups survive the evening.

'Butterflies, aren't those the ugly brainless insects with huge flapping wings that fly about doing nothing and die in a week or two?' the mole enquired.

Like you do anything worthwhile to entitle you to criticise anyone.

'Yes, you're quite right,' the mouse nodded quickly, forgetting the mole's disability. She was too busy watching his flailing paws. 'Oh, let me get that for you,' she said, took the cup from him and set it on the table herself.

'I wouldn't call them brainless, exactly. They have more heart than some beings I know...' Etta said and looked pointedly at the mole. 'But they do have huge, wonderful wings, all the colours of the rainbow...'

'Fui! The rainbow! Don't get me started on the rainbow!' the mole said.

'Just tell the story,' the mouse hissed at Etta, who obliged just to avoid further bitching and moaning.

When Etta finished her tale about the gambling butterflies the mole shrugged, 'The story is quite incredible and therefore simply must be untrue and I'm not sure how I feel about such a vivid imagination,' the mole said.

Lucky you, you don't have to FEEL anything about my imagination. Besides, it was all true! But I cannot convince fools who refuse to believe because they lack similar experiences.

The mole continued undeterred by Etta's train of thought, '...but I still like the sweet melody I hear in your voice, child,' the mole addressed the cupboard while Etta stood at the far end of the kitchen, washing up. 'Even if you do tell lies,' The mole finished and Etta wanted to stick a fork in him.

She managed an 'Uh-huh...' through gritted teeth and continued with her scrubbing.

'She's a pretty little thing too,' the mouse quickly added.

Wait, what? The Missus just paid her a compliment? Really?

Why?

'I'm sure she is, I'm sure she is,' the mole said, 'Now, it's late and I must retire, Missus Mouse.' He stuck out his paw, narrowly missing a cup on the table, 'My light, if you please!'

The mouse stifled a gasp and scurried to fetch him his cane but not before she personally carried all her favourite china to the kitchen. 'Here you are, Mister Mole, here you are! Come back tomorrow!' she said, handing him a lantern and ushering him out into the darkness that linked their two households.

Oh, I certainly hope not, Etta thought.

Count me out!

She had to get away.

Anything was better than another evening of complaints and being called a liar.

***

Before bedtime, the mouse requested more tea. Wondering where all that tea went, Etta dosed the mouse again and started counting the minutes until she could be alone in peace and quiet to figure out what she needed to take and wear for her trek over to the wall.

'The woods...they used to be so alive, you know?' the mouse said wistfully. 'My husband, he was the first to be taken...then it was the neighbours...'

'Then the hedgehogs,' Etta muttered to herself.

'What's that? Yes, then the hedgehogs who used to scurry around delivering everybody's messages, then one day there were no more animals in the underbrush. No more birds of prey either and that was a bit alarming at first... Then, thankfully I discovered Mister Mole was also spared and I was relieved...' the mouse nodded off.

Etta looked at the mouse and furrowed her brow.

The mouse had just parroted the same story, word for word, that she had told Etta the night Etta had wanted to leave and didn't.

Word for word.

Strange.

The mouse had sounded like the old woman when she had been telling Etta the same fairy-tales over and over again.

How many times had the mouse told that story?

Only once to Etta, ok, maybe a few times to Daisy before, but it sounded memorised word for word as if told and retold again and again.

Was everything the mouse had told her that night just a story?

'My babies,' the mouse muttered and went back to sleep.

Could she have done it on purpose to elicit pity so Etta wouldn't leave that night?

Questions on top of questions and nobody to discuss them with.

Well, that was about to change, Etta hoped.

She snuggled into the woollen throw, picked up her satchel with supplies and climbed out the window.

Chapter 24. The Boot

When Etta reached her destination, she saw half a wand sticking out of the wall right where Caroline had come through before.

A manual solution?

Nice!

Etta took hold of the wand and crossed over.

Caroline's cottage beckoned from afar.

Also, it was much warmer this side of the wall.

Etta smiled, thrust her throw into her satchel and set off towards the cottage.

'Hello! I've been expecting you!' said Caroline almost in a sing-song when Etta knocked and entered, stifling a gag.

'Thank you for sticking the wand in the wall. You know, I think this is definitely a better way for us to get together compared to the initial one you tried,' Etta said, breathing as little as she could. She looked around. All the windows were closed, the drapes were drawn, an assortment of pots and pans was littering the kitchen and everything was covered with a thin layer of dust.

The only spotless place was the huge oak table where Caroline, all skin and bone, was sitting in front of the spell-book.

Someone had been busy.

'Yes, I don't fancy seeing your bare bottom again, darling,' Caroline squinted her nose.

'Then perhaps you shouldn't have summoned me without checking what I was doing first,' Etta coloured to her roots and stuck a tongue out to cover up her embarrassment.

Crouching down in the bushes and finding herself in the middle of Caroline's living room had been awkward. Thank goodness she hadn't done anything yet!

'How did you do that anyway?' Etta asked, discovering that she could almost tolerate the stench if she kept breathing through her mouth.

'With a spell,' Caroline looked coy and tapped the book in front of her.

Etta's eyes goggled, 'You and spells? Pray tell!'

'After we did the learning to read spell, I've been trying to learn all sorts of spells, and while my spell-book is useful, oddly, it has only the very basic spells. Like for a five-year old.' Caroline smiled. 'Anyway, I had to start inventing spells. And it wasn't a summoning spell I tried, I tried a revealing spell and it did reveal lots, more than I wanted, actually, but it was just for a moment and we've got a long way before you or I can travel through a magic mirror which allows one to walk between places,' she said.

'A wormhole,' Etta said, remembering her talks with the old woman.

'No, no, there are no worms involved, I can assure you,' Caroline had her nose in the spell-book.

'No, what I meant was the passageway between your abode and mine is a wormhole, that's what they call them,' Etta explained.

'They?' Caroline asked.

'Well, my mother did, anyway,' Etta said.

'Your mother? You are fortunate enough to know your mother? Really? What was she like? Was she kind? Was she beautiful? I assume she was because you are a little... I wish I knew my mother...'

Etta observed Caroline fade into a dream world of her own.

'My mother was a human woman of about thirty-five, childless, single by choice and living on a steady diet of television and gardening,' Etta said. 'She was nice to me, we had lots of fun and good talks. She was a good educator, I guess...'

'While television sounds tasty,' Caroline said, 'you said she was human. Are you part-human too? I thought you were the same as me, a fairy? Well, almost the same as me,' Caroline fluttered her wings, the only undead thing about her.

'Show-off,' Etta said, wishing she had wings, too. 'No, I'm not human. Otherwise I would be a different size,' Etta said.

'Then how did you end up with a mother?' Caroline asked slyly.

Etta shrugged, 'I don't know. I lived with her all my life, I think. She told me she asked a witch for a child, any child and she got me and she was happy, even though I wasn't her size. She said it was even better that I was tiny...' Etta said as Caroline furrowed her brow so much so that half of it fell off.

Caroline didn't even notice. 'The bit about someone being happy that I was tiny - mind you, pesky but tiny - sounds awfully familiar, I just don't know why...' She said.

Oh my, Caroline's memory was going.

Before she forgot everything altogether...

'Caroline, how well do you remember the Fairy Queen?' Etta asked as she made them some tea, washing everything carefully first.

'Why?' Caroline asked.

'When you first met her, she promised to come back and transport you to somewhere you would be happy. Did you get to know her while she brought you here?' Etta enquired.

'When she came back, she fussed about my not having the proper clothes... She nearly forced me to strip naked then and there in the underbrush. I had to firmly tell her I would do no such thing until we reached my new lodgings,' Caroline said.

'And how did she take you talking back at her?' Etta asked.

Caroline shrugged, 'She just smiled and nodded and agreed that undressing is best done in private. She didn't say much thereafter, just flew me here, handed me the spell-book without even making sure I was able to read it, said something about urgent errands and flew off and I haven't seen her since...'

So the queen didn't like being contradicted. Not by anyone. Etta remembered the queen's attitude towards the bugs. *Why else had she clammed up and never returned?*

Etta looked at Caroline who was delicately sipping her tea, perched upright in her armchair like an exotic bird. She took a cookie and dipped it into the tea. Etta saw Caroline's finger-tip touch the surface. When Caroline lifted her hand, the tip of her index finger had melted off. Caroline either didn't notice or pointedly ignored the fact of her decomposition.

Still, the Fairy Queen had brought Caroline back to a semblance of a life...

She could have just let her rot.

Instead, she had given her a wand and wings, new lodgings and extended her life by a little while.

Caroline swallowed her cookie and asked, 'Instead of asking me about persons you've never met, why don't you help me figure out this spell....' She tapped her spell-book.

Deep in thought Etta had forgotten to breathe through her mouth and regretted it as the stench wafted towards her with every tap.

'If we're going to pore over spells again... When was the last time you aired the room?' Etta walked over to the windows and threw them wide.

'Oh no....' She heard Caroline gasp from behind her and saw her dart to the furthest recesses of the room, covering herself up as best as she could.

'What? What'd I do? Are you scared you'll catch a cold or something?' Etta said. *She doubted the undead could catch colds.*

She also doubted fresh air could make Caroline decompose quicker than she already was. She wasn't even going to feel the breeze all the way over there.

From the corner, two murky pools of water glistened at Etta, 'You opened that because of the smell, didn't you? I know it smells in here and it's disgusting, it's just that I feel like taking flight and being sucked out with the wind every time I'm near a window...and...and...it gets worse...' Caroline's squeaky voice dropped to a whisper, '...the awful smell that you smell...' she sniffled, '...I can no longer smell it at all...'

Etta processed the information and asked the obvious question, 'Your sense of smell is gone?'

Thank heavens! At least the smell of decay wouldn't be bothering one of them anymore.

Etta closed the window, leaving it ajar enough for pure air to at least seep in.

Caroline poured them tea and sat down. 'I knew it smelled funny in here before...when I could smell.'

You think?

'And I know that my senses giving up on me is not a good sign...' Caroline said and placed her hands in her lap.

'And I know it's a blessing that there are no mirrors here, because I think I look a bit funny....' Caroline continued, glancing at her missing fingertip and then concentrating on plucking at the lace sleeve at her frayed wrist instead.

Etta thought Caroline was starting to look more and more like the lace she wore - delicate egg-white and almost translucent.

Caroline looked straight at Etta, 'You know what's wrong with me, don't you?' she asked, telegraphing with her whole being that all she wanted was reassurance that nothing was wrong with her.

I'm going to tell her when bigger bits start falling off, Etta decided. *Then she'll have to accept her fate. Until then, needless worry is not going to help.*

Etta took a cup, 'This tea is delicious! What's in it?'

Caroline rolled her eyes, 'Stop changing the subject!'

Etta smiled, 'What subject? So, you're worried about your looks, who isn't? Come to think of it, you're a bit preoccupied with that. You have nothing to worry about. You look lovely. So, stop obsessing about it, ok? As for the smell thing? You know when food is burnt just by looking at it. So, you won't go hungry. And as for not smelling the smell that used to be here...'

Is still here, but neveryoumind...

'...I'll make you a deal - you stop worrying about smelling things and I'll tell you when it smells in here when I visit and we can air the room or maybe even go and search for and get rid of the smelly thing...'

Finding an old shoe or somesuch and making Caroline believe this was the source of the smell should not be a problem anymore now that Caroline couldn't smell.

'...and it won't smell here anymore and then it shouldn't matter that you cannot smell things, right?' Etta proposed as Caroline nodded.

'You mean you think so too, that there is a smelly thing, like a stinky old boot or something, and you'll help me find it?' Caroline blinked. 'You wouldn't mind?'

Etta looked at her and nodded.

How do you tell your friend that she IS the smelly thing? Answer: you don't. Not unless you want to lose said friend.

Right, time to find that stinky old boot.

Etta sincerely hoped someone else besides Caroline had lived in this place before so there would be old boots to find.

An hour after, they had found and burnt an old boot and Etta felt accomplished enough to dare broach more serious subjects.

Like Caroline being the undead and how they both got to this neck of the woods.

Etta plopped herself down in the dusty armchair and heard a squeak.

She fished out the thing pressing against her back.

The leather-bound spell-book.

The leather must have creaked when she sat on it.

'Ooh, goody. Let's see about that spell now...' Caroline said craning her neck and Etta rolled her eyes. 'I couldn't make out this word. I mean, I can read now, but I don't know how to pronounce this,' Caroline said pointing at a word. 'What is it, eks-see-o, eks-chi-o...'

'Eks-ski-o,' Etta said, reading 'excio'. 'What did you want to evoke?'

'Not what, who. You,' Caroline said. 'I tried saying it everywhich way I could think of and for a second it showed me you and then nothing.'

'You said *excio Etta* and saw me?' Etta asked, incredulous that spells could be so easy.

'Well, no...' Caroline bit her lip, 'I said *eks-see-o nympharum*, then I thought this was too generic, so I said *eks-see-o nympharum ego ocurrit* and then I got to *invoco nympharum sine alas cum niger capillum* and then I caught a glimpse of you, well your bare bottom rather, but...'

Etta rolled her eyes, 'You tried 'evoke fairy', then 'evoke fairy I have met' and then 'summon fairy without wings with black hair'...why didn't you just use my name?'

Caroline looked down, toed the rug and said in a small voice, 'Because I forgot...'

15. *.She sighed and carried the tea pot into the living room. Later, she'd dose the tea later.*

Chapter 25. The Logic

'You forgot my name?!?' Etta gaped, 'You…forgot…my name?!? Really?'

Maybe Caroline's brain was decaying with the rest of her…

'Funnily enough, the generic spells didn't summon the Fairy Queen, although she is also a fairy I have met….' Caroline said.

'You are side-tracking,' Etta said.

'I'm sorry, ok?' Caroline said. 'I'm sorry I forgot your name… and didn't manage to come up with a decent spell to get in touch sooner… I haven't been feeling myself lately…' she said and sat herself delicately down into an armchair. She looked so pathetic and frail, perched there, that Etta didn't have the heart to chide her.

'My name is Etta. Write it down, just in case you forget again. And apology accepted.'

Caroline nodded happily, 'I won't forget anymore, I promise! Will you help me get the spell right? So we have a means of communication when you leave…do you have to leave? I mean you could live here…and help me not forget…' her voice trailed off as her eyes found the window.

Etta followed her gaze.

We couldn't air the room because it would blow your papyrus-thin skin off and if we didn't open the window, then I couldn't stay long because of the smell. At night, I'd suffocate in the stench or drown in my own vomit.

Out loud she said, 'Caroline, this is a lovely offer, it really is and thank you for being so kind…I just cannot leave the mouse at the moment for longer than a few days…' Etta said and told Caroline about the mouse's life before the fairies, fully knowing she was using it as a distraction as much as an explanation.

'She sounds like she needs you watching over her more than I do…' Caroline said.

Etta shrugged.

At the rate Caroline was decaying, that was debatable.

Out loud she said, 'Well, the mouse and her best friend, the mole, are pathetic and annoying, but they are harmless...'

Caroline straightened in her chair, 'So, you don't think I'm pathetic or annoying? Yay!'

Etta raised an eyebrow at that deduction, but didn't say anything.

Caroline prattled on, 'I get it, you need to go keep an eye on the mouse so she doesn't do any harm to herself. You'll be babysitting. I don't need babysitting. I just like some company now and again. You'll be there and I'll be here, which means we do need to come up with a way to keep in touch.'

Etta smiled.

Dog with a bone.

'Next time you could say Excio Etta,' Etta said. 'Let's try, shall we?' she said and went into the other room. 'Now say it!' she yelled.

'Eks-ski-o Etta!' Caroline yelled and Etta observed the wall between the two rooms become transparent. Caroline's happy face stared back at her. 'Excellent!' Caroline said and clapped her hands together.

'Oh, good, it works, the sound as well, not just the picture,' Etta said, 'Great!'

'You have to use a verb followed by a noun - or a name in your case - and tell the thing that you want to happen - to happen,' Caroline said.

'Nouns, verbs, a few months ago you didn't know how to read,' Etta muttered fingering the wand in her apron pocket. Then she registered what Caroline had just said. 'Wait, you're saying there is a definite logic to spells and as long as one knows Latin...' Etta brightened.

'Oh, it's a bit more complicated than that,' Caroline said. 'Why else do you think I've been having trouble getting through to you?'

'Bad pronunciation?' Etta suggested walking over to where Caroline was just in time to see Caroline stick the tip of her tongue out.

If she stuck it all out, it might fall off and by the looks of it, Caroline was a bit more aware of her demise than she let on.

'So, teach me, oh wise Enchantress,' Etta bowed.

Caroline laughed and clapped her hands again, 'This is going to be so much fun!' She rose carefully from her armchair. 'First, it doesn't matter which comes first, the verb or the noun, but it usually is a verb and a noun, occasionally an adverb as well - your basic who does what how...'

'So, where's the tricky part?' Etta asked.

'The tricky part is knowing the precise thing that you want to happen and telling that thing itself to make it happen,' Caroline said. 'I've been itching to try if compelling spells would work on living beings...' she said, eyeing Etta with a greedy glint in her eyes.

'No, you are not going to compel me to do anything before you teach me how to defend myself,' Etta said, snatching away Caroline's wand.

Caroline pouted, 'Very well. Defence spells are even trickier, because you have to use pronouns... Try this - point my wand at something and tell that thing to protect you by saying 'Protegas me!''

Etta said 'Protegas me!' to a table, which hopped up and rose on its hind legs in between Etta and Caroline.

'I think it senses your harmful thoughts,' Etta said peeking around the table.

Caroline rolled her eyes and had to knock herself on the side of the head to make them fall back properly.

Back to the logic of spells.

'So I need to tell things or living beings to do specific things for a specific purpose using Latin and my wand?' Etta asked.

'Here, let me show you!' Caroline said.

'*Convenio linteum quadratum!*' she said to the bits of fluff that had fallen off her linen decorative pillow. The bits of fluff assembled themselves into a tiny square-shaped linen cloth.

Verb, noun, adjective.

'Let me try,' Etta said and took her wand out, '*Convenio linteum quadratum!*'

She got the same result with the next bits of lint.

It worked!

Her wand worked!

'Oh, you have one as well?' Caroline eyed Etta's wand.

'I kind of inherited it,' Etta said. 'It belonged to someone else but was left for me to find. To be honest, I wasn't able to use it for anything. For all practical purposes, back at the mouse's, it was just a pretty blue stick. This is the first time it has actually done anything!'

'Maybe you needed proper spells for it to work?' Caroline suggested. 'Come on, let's try a few more!'

After half an hour of Etta repeating all the spells Caroline tried, Etta was confident nothing was wrong with her wand at all when proper spells were used. Etta decided to ask what she had been itching to ask from the very beginning, 'Is there a spell to transport me back?'

Caroline's face grew sad, 'That's the one I've been trying to come up with for months now. It involves too many variables - telling you, your body, brain, fluids, thoughts, wand and everything to go somewhere specific, in a specific location and telling that location to accept your movement and telling time to cooperate and telling the colours not to change and telling the void left behind to close...that's as far as I got and still nothing,' Caroline said and sniffled.

Before the waterworks started, they needed a win.

Etta rifled her brain for a spell that would make Caroline happy.

The book coughed loudly on the table where they had left it.

'Any help would be much appreciated,' Etta whispered to it goggling her eyes at Caroline.

The book flipped open.

Etta eyed it thoughtfully.

Whaddaya know. Magic books could help if they really wanted to.

Etta read the title of the spell out loud, '*Incantatum perpetuus donec confringetur* - a lasting spell until it's broken,' Etta said.

'What does that mean?' Caroline asked.

'A lasting spell...a lasting spell,' Etta mumbled to herself.

A lasting spell and Caroline...to prevent her skin falling off...no, she would just look horrible with dead skin stuck to her face...probably the only way to reverse Caroline being undead was to let her die...

So how else could Etta help with a permanent spell...

A lasting spell to help Caroline...

She was living through a perpetual ground-hog day and would continue to do that for however long her semblance of a life would last...

Hang on...hang on...

'Got it!' she beamed. 'You can use a lasting spell to get out of your Enchantress duties!'

Caroline looked at her with suspicion, 'How?'

Etta studied the spell. 'If I'm reading this right, we have to enchant the subject to be in one permanent shape and tie an object to the spell while we are at it and put a time-stamp on it too. Basically tie a thing and the person together for however long the thing lasts...' Etta looked at Caroline's hopeful face.

'What are you saying?' Caroline blinked.

'The Beast will be a beast all the time and you won't have to re-enact the day he made the wrong decision over and over again!' Etta said and asked, 'Does the prince have a cat or a dog?'

Caroline looked startled, 'Wh...what? Does the spell involve some sort of animal sacrifice, because I'm not going to...'

Etta rolled her eyes, 'No sacrifice.' She showed the spell-book to Caroline, 'See, here...We'll have to tie the spell to a living thing. Animals live longer than plants. If he has a cat or a dog, we can make the spell last for ten years. He's fifteen, right? Ten years would be enough to allow him to grow up a little if he doesn't have to repeat one day over and over again.'

Caroline shook her head, 'No cat or dog.'

Etta tap-tapped her chin, 'Hm, then we'll have to tie the spell to a plant, I guess...'

'How long would that last?' Caroline asked.

'Six years.'

'Rose bushes live for tens of years,' Caroline offered. 'There were roses under my window when I was growing up...'

Etta looked up and noticed cut-off roses in one of the vases. 'A rose...' she said. 'How long has that one been there?'

Caroline shrugged, 'Dunno, it was already here by the time I moved in.'

Months.

OK, even when cut-off roses managed to survive for months in Caroline's wood.

'Ok, a rose it is,' Etta nodded.

'I like roses,' Caroline chimed in.

'A rose is probably better than a cat, anyway. The Beast can easily keep it safe, whereas imagine having to guard the cat so it doesn't jump off somewhere and die,' Etta mumbled, pouring over the spell-book as Caroline fumbled with her sleeve.

'The only catch is...'

'There's a catch?' Caroline echoed, looking up.

Etta gave Caroline 'the eye', 'You should know better than anyone there is always a catch.'

Caroline nodded, 'So, what's the catch?'

Etta read the page backwards and forwards, hoping she was wrong.

'I'm not sure I understand this well... Either casting he spell that ties the Beast to the rose will permanently release the caster - you - from related duties... I'm assuming this means you acting like the Enchantress every day... OR permanent release of the caster will make the spell also permanent... I can only assume permanent release of the caster means death...'

'I don't get it,' Caroline said.

'Either you are free to go permanently or if you should die, the Beast will be Beast permanently. It seems that with this particular spell, caster's death would not lift the spell, quite the contrary. But in any case, you will have six years to frolick around, doing whatever you like. How does that sound?' Etta looked at Caroline, bright-eyed and bushy-tailed.

'But if the spell lasts six years if tied to a plant, how can it be made permanent until the six years are up?' Caroline asked.

Etta doubted Caroline would last six years.

Etta thought about it, 'I think the spell is meant to be lifted after the six years are up, but if you're not there anymore, the spell could be made permanent, if nobody comes and disenchants the boy in six years. That's the way I understand it.'

Caroline nodded slowly.

'Because a girl would have to come along and fall in love and kiss the Beast in Beast form before his six years are up,' Etta said, trying not to pity the Beast.

Because if no girl came during six years, then with Caroline dead long before, the Beast would be Beast forever. Well, she assumed permanently meant forever. Or until he died of old age...

'It would have to be a girl kind enough not to care about being lured here,' Caroline mused. 'I haven't left the woods so I couldn't look around properly, but I'm sure there's a nearby village - I mean the food for the castle and my home just appears, but it has to come from somewhere. So I'm fairly sure I will be able to find a girl interested to come and meet the prince...' Caroline said. 'It worked for me. I'd disenchant him myself, except I don't think I'm meant to. I mean, I don't think he's meant for me...' she sighed and scratched her elbow. 'I'm sure I can find a girl sooner than six years, but only if I don't have to be stuck here every morning cursing the poor boy, you know!'

'You'll be free to start looking as soon as we cast the spell,' Etta said. 'When the spell is tied to the rose, you won't have to be here anymore, which means you will be free to go anywhere and do anything you like. After you find a girl, that is.' Etta said and noticed Caroline's skin was flaking badly where she had scratched herself.

Hell, she definitely wouldn't last six years if this was her rate of decay over ten months.

Etta didn't know whether to tell Caroline that continuing the daily routine which couldn't last beyond Caroline's complete decay would be kinder than tying the boy's fate to a flower. *For eternity, as it may be. Because a girl randomly wading into a castle and taming the Beast with love after Caroline was gone was...well...just a story.*

Then again, there was no guarantee that the queen would not send someone else after Caroline was gone to keep torturing the boy until the lesson was properly learnt.

Caroline nodded, 'I don't think I'd last six years anyway,' she said and looked at Etta. She removed a flap of her skin revealing bone.

Etta tried not to flinch.

'I'm decaying, in case you haven't noticed.'

An uneasy silence settled.

'I don't think it was that boot after all that caused the smell. It was me all along, but thank you for being kind and sticking by me no matter how I smell,' Caroline said and lowered her eyes.

A lonely tear trickled down her parchment-white cheek.

'Hang on, hang on. So, ok, you're decaying a bit. But look at the bright side. We'll tie the Beast to a rose with a spell and you'll have room to roam and you now know the *Excio* spell and if you should have trouble remembering my name or pronouncing things, then we now know that sticking the wand into the wall as a means of communication also works, that's all a good start, right?' Etta said to comfort Caroline. 'And if we are now both going to be working on the transportation spell, then I am sure we'll succeed, sooner or later, right?'

Caroline nodded and sniffled, swiping the tear away with a practised flick of her silk handkerchief. 'Marriage at fifteen is bordering on the illegal anyway...,' she muttered. 'Especially to that tantrum-throwing child! Six years in one form and avoiding the same day repeating over and over again will hopefully do him and his temper some good.'

'So we tie his fate to this rose?' Etta asked and fingered the thorny specimen in Caroline's vase.

Caroline nodded, 'Let's try!'

'You wouldn't know if it works until the next morning.'

'That's ok,' Caroline said.

Next, Etta proposed to work on the transportation spell.

It turned out to be more difficult than anticipated.

When Etta left the next day, they were no closer to cracking it than Caroline had been by herself.

Still, Caroline was in much better spirits.

They had agreed on having tea and cakes in a week's time.

Life couldn't be better - her wand worked with proper spells, no disenchantment necessary, she knew how to make spells even without a book and she had made sure Caroline repeated the *Excio* spell a few times and wrote down Etta's name.

Wrapped in her throw, Etta happily trekked back through the snow to the house the mouse had built.

Chapter 26. Bacon and Alzheimer's

Etta found the mouse's house thoroughly trashed.

Without Etta to keep her stable did Missus Mouse have one of her episodes again?

Etta tsk-tsked and started cleaning, mumbling, 'How can anybody go this nuts? It's like she goes all animal...'

Etta fluffed the decorative pillows on the bed.

Oh, how she'd come to hate these pillows!

Removing a scrap of bacon from the lamp, Etta looked at it.

They had had bacon for breakfast the day before Etta had left for Caroline's and the mouse had made her put the scraps in the compost.

Had she fished these out from outside?

But that would make her tantrums...deliberate.

If you were going to go nuts, you would just trash what was around you. Not fetch something from outside and then trash everything.

Or had she been fetching the scraps from outside, come in and had a tantrum while the scraps were still in her paws?

Still, why would she fetch the scraps from outside?

Etta looked at the bacon closely.

Crispy.

Had the mouse been...recycling?!?

Etta gagged.

How many times had they eaten that particular bit of bacon for breakfast?

Vowing to stay off the meats and check what was really in their pantry, Etta had another thought.

Scraps...and eating anything ...well...edible...that was more rat behaviour.

Animalistic.

Missus Mouse was an animal.

Why had she ruled out basic instincts just because in this nook of the magic forest animals spoke and were sentient?

She had even explained the berserk episodes away as grief over the loss of everyone the mouse had ever loved.

What if the berserk episodes were simply the mouse's basic self returning?

Etta hadn't heard of rabies being spread through mice, but the Black Plague had spread through fleas on rats...

Maybe she should start dosing the mouse during the day as well?

It would be easier for her to overpower a groggy mouse rather than a fully alert aggressive one.

Then and there, Etta regretted saying no to Caroline.

She had only said no because of the smell and because she had thought the mouse and mole to be harmless.

Now she wondered...

Maybe the smell wouldn't be so bad after all.

Compared with being afraid for her life, Caroline's stench seemed almost tolerable.

Making a mental note not to agitate the Missus, Etta made sure the house was spic and span, which was how her landlady liked it.

When the mouse returned and saw Etta, she froze.

Oh good, better that she's afraid of me than me of her, Etta thought.

'Back, are you?' was all that the mouse said.

She had been absent for five days and that was the welcome back she got?

'Missed me, did you?' Etta retorted, motioning around. 'I cleaned up as you can see.'

'That's your job,' the mouse dropped curtly.

'What went wrong this time? Did you remember your husband again and the grief got to you?' Etta asked, almost forgiving the mouse for trashing the place. The old woman used to say that when you understood why people - and perhaps mice - did horrible things, you couldn't hate them for being horrible anymore.

'What are you talking about? I have no husband,' the mouse said.

'Yes, but you had one. You told me yourself,' Etta said.

'I did no such thing!' the mouse wriggled her whiskers.

Etta looked the mouse over from head to toe. It seemed to be the same mouse who had been her landlady the past few months, down to the apron and that brown spot under her eye.

Easy there. Nobody came in and switched mice while I was away.

Etta pointed to the nail next to the door where the key hung, 'A little while ago you told me that you met your husband, had a wedding, wed by the Fairy Queen, no less, and he was taken the morning after, with the key still hanging where it had been, with his tea cup still warm and without any note explaining where he went or why he had to go.'

The mouse kept twitching her whiskers. 'Tea, I need tea,' she finally squeaked.

'Are you saying I imagined all that?' Etta asked.

'I'm...I'm not saying anything of the sort but yes, I think you must have dreamt it!' The mouse brightened. 'That's it! It's like one of your stories, pure imagination and you do have a vivid one!'

Etta gaped.

Ooh-kay. For some reason the mouse didn't want to admit she had spilled the beans.

As the mouse was fussing with her decorative pillows, Etta went to the kitchen to make tea.

'Mister Mole is indisposed today, he won't be joining us,' the mouse said from behind her, making Etta jump.

'Sheesh, you scared me!' She said, nearly dropping the pot.

As the mouse stayed to fuss with the cups, Etta was unable to add a few drops of her super secret formula.

She sighed and carried the tea pot into the living room.

Later, she'd dose the tea later.

This way, she could have a cup herself.

Etta poured and took up one of the armchairs, leaving the one the mole favoured for the Missus.

The mouse looked lost for a second, then plopped herself down, nearly disappearing into the dilapidated cushions. She perched herself on the edge of the chair and took up her cup from the table as if nothing had happened.

Etta caught the mouse stealing glances at the legs of the armchair that by now were sticking out at curious angles.

Too frequent wear and tear by someone whose weight the chair was not meant to carry.

'So, what did you get up to while I was away?' Etta asked, trying to keep up the conversation.

'You were away?' The mouse looked surprised.

Etta snorted into her tea.

The mouse couldn't have been out cold for five days.

It had taken Etta two days to trek to the wall and the same time to come back. Plus she had spent a day with Caroline.

Had the mouse been away as well this whole time?

Or, given her previous denial, was the mouse simply having memory problems?

'If I start finding your socks stashed with the cutlery, that's when I'll know you have Alzheimer's...' Etta mumbled.

Luckily, memory was easy to test.

'Do you remember when you were growing up?'

'What?' The mouse turned to her and blinked.

'When you were little? I mean did you always love tea? Were you always inquisitive? Did your family teach you to be kind to strangers? Did you always love guests? That kind of thing,' Etta said.

The mouse's paw froze with the cup halfway to her mouth. 'Erm...no...?' She said.

Etta cursed herself for asking too many questions. She distinctly remembered the old woman telling her that that was the surest way to confuse someone and get no answer at all or get only the last question answered.

Etta sighed, 'No you didn't always love tea or no you don't remember?' she asked.

'What are you interrogating me for?' The mouse bristled.

'I'm just asking,' Etta shrugged.

'Why? Why are you asking? Nobody before...' the mouse said and clammed up.

'Nobody before did what - asked questions?' Etta enquired.

The mouse glared.

'Oh, give it up! You called me Daisy when we met, remember?' Etta said.

'I did no such thing!' the mouse said and wriggled her whiskers.

Etta blinked.

But there was a Daisy.

There had been.

The question was - why would the mouse lie about it?

There had to be a good reason.

Just like there had to be a good reason for why the mouse refused to answer questions about her childhood or pretended she never told Etta about her husband.

Maybe she truly didn't remember.

Nodding slowly, Etta took the pot and went to the kitchen for refills.

Tea.

Spiked tea.

It had worked as a truth-serum once.

Maybe it would work its magic again and the Missus would relax and tell all without Etta having to pry.

Chapter 27. The Wonky Wand

Etta yanked at the door and gave it a good kick.

Yesterday, the mouse had kept quiet and tea just put her to sleep.

Now, the mouse had accidentally locked her in?

If this was Alzheimer's, it was progressing.

Etta eyed the nail where the key usually hung and pouted.

There was no use trying the door handle again.

Locked was locked was locked.

Except...

Etta smiled happily and fished out her wand.

Verb, noun.

'*Porta apertum!*' Etta pointed at the key hole.

Not 'open door'?

Maybe it was the hinges that she needed to address?

'*Aperta cardine!*' Etta said.

Did the hinges themselves need to evaporate?

'*Cardine evanesco?*' Etta suggested.

Still nothing.

She tried various spells she could come up with, down to 'whatever thing that needs to move to let me out of here' to no avail.

Her Latin wasn't that rusty.

Why didn't her wand want to help her?

Did it even work?

It was easy enough to test.

Etta looked around.

She tried a spell to repair a broken cup, just like Caroline had done. '*Restituo calix!*' she said and pointed at the delicate China cup the mouse had dropped yesterday.

The cup assembled itself back without a crack to be seen.

Her wand worked!

Etta tried another spell she remembered very well, 'Excio Caroline!' she said and prepared herself to savour Caroline's surprise.

Nothing happened.

Etta was puzzled.

There was nothing wrong with her pronunciation.

Wait a minute...

First, the door spell, now this one?

They had spent the best part of an hour drilling 'Excio Etta' into Caroline.

Oh.

SHE had never tried 'Excio Caroline' with her own wand.

To be sure, Etta tried various other spells she had copied after Caroline.

Half an hour later, all the trash in the house had evaporated, her nightshade was blooming again, all of Etta's clothes were mended and she was sadly sure of one thing.

This side of the wall, her wand could only do spells it had done before.

Old dog, no new tricks.

Which meant there were no means for her to communicate with Caroline.

Again.

Not unless she trekked there, which she should do anyway in a few days, like they agreed.

Except...

She was locked in until the mouse came back.

Or maybe not...

She needn't even try the window in the kitchen.

She couldn't get the planks unstuck.

The window had been open throughout the summer.

At the first sight of snow, the mouse had procured two wooden planks and nailed the window shut.

Etta didn't think she would miss staring at the ferns when doing the dishes, but staring at the wooden planks for weeks was slowly getting to her.

She was definitely locked in until the mouse came back.

Now Etta really regretted that she hadn't asked Caroline to disenchant her wand.

This useless, stupid wand that could only parrot the spells it already knew!

16.   Spiked tea. It had worked as a truth-serum once.

Chapter 28. The Bird

Etta was so out of sorts over her wand that she pointedly ignored the mouse when she returned the next day.

The mouse had either not noticed or didn't care about Etta's moody silence, chatting away with the mole who had materialised the second the mouse arrived.

It was as if he had been lurking behind their back door all along, Etta bristled.

She had cooked and cleaned and fetched them tea all evening without uttering a single word.

Not that anyone had noticed.

When the mole had finally decided to go, the mouse handed Etta a lantern, 'You carry it, girl!'

'We're seeing our guest home in person now, are we?' Etta asked, trying to disguise her excitement.

She was going to be allowed to explore!

Etta tried hard to look disinterested.

The back door opened to pitch black.

The mole was the first to go.

Etta followed, wanting to push the mouse out of her way.

She scoped out the surroundings while trying to keep up with the mole.

They were in a tunnel!

Was there just the one or were there more branches?

Etta steadied herself, touching the wall.

The faint glow the lantern was emitting was enough to stop her from stumbling, but not to see far ahead.

The tunnel seemed round, except for the floor. The walls sloped unevenly.

Burrowed.

Probably by the mole.

Their shadows moved listlessly beside them as they walked on.

Once, a cobweb fluttered down and settled on Etta's shoulder.

Etta shivered.

Next time, she'll take a blanket.

If there was going to be a next time.

Etta saw the mole squeeze past a mountain of dirt blocking the pathway.

The mouse pressed herself against the wall and edged by the formation, taking small steps.

Curious about whether this was a cave-in and whether this meant there was a hole up top, Etta approached the mound.

She saw a stick ending in three twigs.

When she shone some light on it, it looked a lot like a leg of a bird.

Then she spotted the ink-black feathers.

To make sure, she brushed her hand over the mound.

Soft.

She walked on and came up to the head of the bird.

A swallow!

Its eyes were closed.

Feeling a breeze, Etta looked for the source.

Just like that, she was staring at millions of diamonds in the ink-black sky.

Stars!

How long had it been that she hadn't seen them?

I seemed ages ago that she had roamed the forest to her heart's content.

The bird trembled, making Etta jump back.

Final contusions?!?

The bird twitched one more time and lay still.

What was she, a magnet for the dead?

'Stop dawdling, girl and fetch the light! I can't see where I'm going!' the mouse ordered from up ahead.

'You could hold the mole's hand,' Etta mumbled but shuffled after them nevertheless.

Unless there was another path back, the mouse and I

will be passing here again and I can have another look if the bird is dead or not.

'Thank you, m'ladies!' the mole said as he set his dandy wooden cane against the wall outside his door.

The cane promptly fell over.

He probably doesn't want his lodgings getting more dirty than necessary, Etta thought.

The mole waved at them and closed the door in their faces.

The mouse grabbed the lantern and frog-marched past the bird and through the tunnels as if the mounds of hell were after her.

I will sneak back after she dozes off, Etta vowed. *After I make her doze off.*

When the nightshade drops had worked their magic, Etta fished the keys from the mouse's pocket.

One of these has got to be the key to the tunnels.

Once she found the right one, she took to the tunnels with the throws, one for her and two more for the bird.

Pointing the lantern in front of her, Etta counted the steps.

Just in case.

At five hundred and twenty-three she saw a familiar stick of a leg.

Etta circled the swallow and put her hand on its head.

Warm.

Barely, but warm.

Etta noticed the bird's short, shallow breaths.

Short and shallow was better than none.

It was alive!

The swallow stirred briefly, in fluttery panic and settled down again when it saw the size of its would-be assailant.

If it has the energy to do that, maybe it's not in such a bad shape after all, Etta thought.

One of the bird's wings lay at a nasty angle that it shouldn't be able to make.

Broken.

The bird opened its eyes again, looked at her glassily and closed them, resigned to its fate.

'You poor thing, you must be cold!' Etta said and used the throws she had brought to cover the bird up.

Two woollen throws barely covered the bird's wings.

Etta took off her throw and lay it on the bird's chest.

It barely covered the bird's heart.

The poor thing could use a lot more than that.

She'd have to improvise.

She would go and fetch the mouse's rug and Etta's bed-throw. And whatever other linen she could find.

Seeing as it was Etta who did the washing, she could say everything in the house had suddenly become dirty and was in the wash. The mouse would be none the wiser.

When it came to, the swallow would also need food and water.

She also needed to doctor the broken wing.

But first things first.

Etta walked the five hundred and twenty-three steps to the mouse's house and then back again, nearly doubled over under the weight of all the linen.

As she heaped all the stuff onto the bird, it didn't even open its eyes.

Etta heard the swallow's breathing become rhythmical and deep.

Good!

It was getting warm.

Right.

Now, on to the mending.

For the wing, she needed two twigs or branches or something more solid to prop it up and hope it would heal.

Etta remembered the mouse had a walking staff for when she ventured into the woods.

That's one twig.

Where would she get another?

Etta remembered the mole's cane outside his door.

Well, now, wasn't that serendipitous.

Picturing the mole's confusion when he finds his cane gone, Etta almost didn't mind the long walk to and fro.

Once the bird healed and could fly away, which was probably in a couple of weeks, Etta could ask to go with it.

With that thought, Etta didn't mind walking back the five hundred and twenty-three steps to get food and water.

When she was done, seeing the pink dawn evict the night sky was her reward.

17. *'The flowers, fui! They always give me the sneezes!'*

Chapter 29. Never Alone

Etta was attacking the pan with a sponge like it was her worst enemy.

The stupid mouse!

The horrid mole!

He was here all day.

From dawn to dusk.

Every day!

The next morning, he had knocked on the tunnel door before she could even go and see if the swallow was feeling better.

There went her chance to see the sun and the sky!

Etta had angrily roused the mouse who had immediately requested tea.

I'll give you tea.

With sleep everlasting, if you and the nasty mole irk me much more today.

Except she couldn't dose the mouse's tea anymore, with the mole constantly there.

Otherwise, they would both doze off and then he'd never leave!

She had to wait until the mole left and the mouse slumbered off before she could go and visit the swallow.

The bird was doing fine. It had opened its eyes and Etta thought it recognised her. She gave it water and a few breadcrumbs, tucked it in and went back to the mouse's to get some sleep.

At dawn, the mole was there again.

She was supposed to be trekking back to Caroline's tomorrow!

Despite the presence of a guest, Missus Mouse had made Etta scrub the kitchen, the floors and even the walls twice that day.

When the mouse ordered her to do it again that same afternoon, first Etta thought she was joking.

She wasn't.

Then Etta thought the mouse's memory was playing up again and she obliged.

It could be because of the visitor - besides muddying the floors he didn't case where he dropped crumbs, napkins and he wasn't the one cleaning up after he spilt his tea.

So the very next day the same routine of pointless scrubbing repeated.

And the next day.

And the next.

The house looked spotless and Etta was dead tired.

There was nothing left to clean, yet the mouse insisted on a twice-daily spring clean routine.

The mole was also quite comfortable escorting himself back, all of a sudden.

Etta hadn't had an opportunity to look in on the bird for a week.

At first, when she had fallen asleep standing in the kitchen, washing up and instead of going to see the bird had dragged herself to her bed, Etta had felt guilty.

The next night, she had started to go, but fell asleep in the tunnels, not ten feet from the mouse's door and had to run back when she heard the mole's shuffle.

She had to face the fact that she was too tired to look after anyone.

She was overworked and constantly tired and NEVER by herself!

'See my face shining in it by the evening!' Etta mimicked the mouse's orders.

Etta threw the pan that refused to get clean into the sink and it clattered loudly.

Where the mouse had found this old thing, was a mystery.

She'd bet anything that the moaning mole was going to

stay until Etta was ready to drop, just like he had this entire week.

'I take comfort in knowing that my tunnels and my abode are my fortress,' the mole said and Etta perked her ears up. *That was probably the most positive thing the mole had ever said during the months that he had been coming here.*

Why he visited, was beyond Etta.

Surely, it wasn't the tea?

He never had anything nice to say nor any news of the world to contribute. All he did was bitch and moan. How the mouse could stand him, she had no idea.

Once, Etta had tried to stick cotton buds in her ears, but was called on pretty quickly.

To avoid her brain exploding from all the moaning, she had started telling them stories instead. At least when she told them about her life with the old woman and about the May bugs, they ooh-ed and aah-ed, but she wasn't entirely convinced they believed her.

The mole had practically called her a liar to her face when she had told him about the forest being cursed and all paths leading back to the oak.

Today, she was all empty on stories and all fed-up by the constant chatting.

What she wouldn't give for a moment of silence and a few extra hours of sleep!

When putting away the mop, Etta noticed a rug near the entrance door.

It was identical to the one she had placed under the swallow's head.

Oh no, she hadn't...

Chapter 30. Gone, Baby, Gone

Etta spent the evening pacing, thinking about the fate of the bird.

If the mouse had taken only the rug away, the swallow should still stay warm with the rest of the stuff Etta had piled on.

She hoped the mole would go soon and they would ask her along again so she could check on her patient.

Instead, the blind bore was dawdling.

'The flowers, fui! They always give me the sneezes,' Mister Mole complained.

'Yes, yes, terrible things they are,' the mouse cooed.

Etta was curious, 'When was the last time you were up top and smelled a flower? ...Mister Mole?' She added for decorum.

There was a lot of huffing and puffing, 'Years ago, actually, but smelling something foul - once is enough, believe me,' he said.

'Yes, you shouldn't contradict your elders, girl!' the mouse admonished as the mole made himself comfortable in his favourite armchair that was sagging closer and closer to the floor with each visit, its legs sporting tiny cracks.

'I wasn't contradicting...I was merely curious. For instance, do you know which flower you happened to smell that made you sneeze? If it was a dandelion, then they only make you sneeze when they are dying and in my experience, most field and forest flowers smell wonderful...' Etta said.

'You're doing it again...' the mouse hissed.

'Doing what?' Etta asked.

'Contradicting your elders.'

Mister Mole fidgeted in the armchair, as much as his girth allowed him to fidget. 'Well, I don't know! I couldn't see it, so how would I know which one it was, but that's not important anyway. Anything up top is foul. Take the sun...'

Before the mole could progress into his usual belittling tirade about the sun Etta said, 'It's not the sun that made you blind, you were born that way. Nature made you that way. You don't need sight deep down in the ground. And vice versa - those of us who do have eyes are meant to see and to enjoy the beauty up top.'

The silence was deafening.

'Stop. Contradicting. Your. Elders.' Missus Mouse had taken Etta by the sleeve and with every word was pulling her towards the kitchen. 'Wash up!' She hissed. 'Now!'

'Are you sure you're my elders? I mean the sheer...' *ignorance* Etta thought, but didn't say, 'How old are you, exactly? I'm fifteen, going on sixteen. How long do mice and moles live, anyway?' She mumbled.

'Khm-khm, I think I'm going to retire for the night, Missus Mouse,' Mister Mole said and slid off the armchair.

Finally!

Who knew complete honesty was refreshingly alienating?

'Oh, so soon, Mister Mole?' The mouse said, fidgeting with her whiskers.

'I think I've overstayed my welcome here...' he huffed, smoothing his velvety coat.

'Oh, no, please don't say that! You're always welcome here! Always!' The mouse assured him, stealing glances at the basket of goodies the gentleman had brought, but he didn't seem to be making gestures towards taking it back. 'I'll talk some sense into the girl, I promise! She'll behave the next time, I promise!' The mouse whispered, quite audibly.

You shouldn't be giving out promises you cannot keep, Etta thought.

'Girl! Take the lantern to show us some light. Mister Mole's retiring for the night!' The mouse ordered.

Etta put down the plate she had been rinsing, quietly happy. 'You want me to escort you back and forth...again?' *If she didn't protest now, perhaps they would suspect something and leave her behind and she couldn't risk that.*

'Don't argue, girl, just do it!' The mouse ordered.

When the mouse opened the door to the tunnels, to her horror Etta saw the mouse's throws and blankets and towels heaped up by the door.

The mouse had retrieved everything, not just the rug...

Poor swallow...

'What's all this? My fresh linen! My kitchen towels that I had just cleaned! Heaped up and all dirty! Who did this?' The mouse squeaked.

Ordered me to clean, actually, Etta bitterly thought.

'Oh, Missus Mouse, I found these in my tunnels and thought perhaps you'd like them back,' the mole said shuffling out the door and taking his cane.

His cane!

Oh, no...

'Oh....oh...thank you, Mister Mole!' the mouse mumbled.

Etta stared at both of them, speechless.

Were they in cahoots or something?

One retrieves her rug, the other the rest of the linen meant to keep the swallow warm.

Quite obviously, they both knew about the bird.

And for now, they were choosing not to ask or then they both already knew how these items had ended up in the tunnels in the first place.

None of this meant anything good for the bird.

Or for Etta, for that matter.

As they made their way down the tunnel, with the mole - for once - gallantly holding up the lantern, Etta's mind raced.

If they both knew about the bird, why did the mouse really need Etta to escort her and the mole?

Did she want to tell her off on site?

She got to counting five hundred steps and her heart started beating even faster.

Twenty-three more.

Fifteen...

Etta saw the light from the lantern fall onto a giant mound of darkness.

Sixteen...

Poor swallow.

Seventeen...

All cold in the dark.

Eighteen...

And who knew for how long.

Nineteen...

Just as it's wing had started to mend.

Twenty...

Etta reached out her hand, almost touching her charge.

Twenty-one...

Twenty-two...

The mouse and the mole walked right past the bird as if it wasn't there.

Twenty-three.

But they SAW it was there?!?

Did they just not care?

Etta noticed the wing lacked the twin-twig prop-up.

Near the beak, Etta stooped down as if to shake out a pebble from her shoe and perked up her ears for any signs of breathing.

'Stop dawdling, girl! Mister Mole is getting tired. Come take the light!' the mouse grumbled.

Etta stood up, resting her hand on the bird's head as if for balance.

The plumage was soft.

Still, it was impossible to tell whether it was alive or dead.

Please don't be dead!

I'll fetch warm stuff as soon as I get rid of these two, Etta mentally promised, taking her torch-bearer's place between the rodents.

By the sound of things, the mouse had pacified the mole, who was walking his usual leisurely wide gait, waving his cane and pointing at things in the passage he couldn't possibly see, but could smell.

There has to be a way to get them to move quicker.

Etta had a thought.

It had worked once before, maybe it would work again?

'Nobody noticed the dead bird back there? Seriously?' Etta asked pointing with the lantern that was glimmering faintly.

'What's that you were saying?' the mole turned and asked, more out of politeness than real interest.

'You take this path every day,' she said to the mole. 'There has been this giant bird lying in the very same passageway and in the very same spot. That neither of you was too happy squeezing past the first time it appeared, which was a week ago,' she said to the mouse. 'Now it's dead,' *I hope not,* 'and you didn't even notice?' Etta asked.

'Bird? What bird?' The mole asked, sounding alarmed.

'Pay her no attention, Mister Mole. As you know, the girl has a vivid imagination,' the mouse said and patted his arm.

A vivid imagination?

You want vivid imagination?

Coming right up!

'The only reason you don't care is because you purposefully lured it here and murdered it!' Etta said, receiving gasps as a reaction.

Good.

'I mean, the bird couldn't have made the hole above it by itself, so you,' Etta poked the mole who flattened himself against the wall, 'dug the hole and lured it in...' she watched the mole closely.

He wasn't even denying it!

'And you,' she glared at the mouse who froze in her spot, 'you took back your rug and left it slightly less warm, that's negligence and...and...manslaughter,' Etta used the word she had heard many a time on the CSI show the old woman had used to watch.

She was pretty sure animals killing birds wasn't any such thing, but they didn't know that.

And you,' she turned back to the mole who raised his cane protectively in front of him and hunched his head in between his shoulders, 'you finished the job by removing every single item of linen that could have kept the poor thing from dying. And took back your stupid cane,' she said, pointing at it. 'So, you two murdered it! That's why you're keeping mum and ignoring the corpse!' Etta said, hoping against hope she was wrong about the corpse thing.

The mouse snickered. 'That's the wildest story we've heard from you yet, girl!' She said and the mole guffawed.

'My name is Etta, not girl!' Etta said as the mouse snatched away the lantern.

'Whatever, we're going and you will come too, unless you want to stay in the dark...with the corpse...' the mouse snickered again.

Etta was horrified.

They knew!

They knew about the bird and had purposefully left it to die and...

She rushed over to the bird and pressed her ear to its heart.

Nothing.

Her bird, her only hope of escaping was...dead.

And the mouse and the mole had known about it.

Worse, they were the ones who had killed it!

Really killed it!

Etta squeezed her knuckles and bit her lip until she drew blood.

The wretched, awful, murderous beasts!

The light from the lantern was fading in the distance.

Her choice at the moment was to stumble back, blind or go after them.

Etta kept biting her lips and started walking.

When she reached the pair of murderers, she had worked herself up to say quite a few things.

As Etta opened her mouth, the mouse ordered, 'Not a word! I know you were abusing my hospitality by feeding my food to that vermin,'

Vermin? Look who's talking!

'...and you dirtied all my pristine laundry and no, I don't forgive you nor am I likely to forget! The trust is gone! Completely gone! I could toss you out the door this second!'

Oh, please do!

'You are lucky I have a kind heart. But if you don't want me to lock you up in the tunnels, then you will not say a word about this whole unfortunate incident ever again!'

Etta closed her mouth in surprise.

She had expected them to be scared of the consequences of their actions.

Regretful, at least.

Certainly not giving her such an ultimatum.

And to think, that for a moment there, she had even been prepared to give them the benefit of a doubt that they, perhaps, did not know what their selfishness would do to the bird!

She had underestimated them both.

They were selfish and cruel, but one thing they were not.

They were definitely NOT stupid.

Maybe they were even cunning.

The faster she got away, the better for her.

After their attention had been lulled, that is.

If she were left in the tunnels by herself...maybe she could climb out of the hole?

Except...

What would she use to make a ladder or a rope or something to hoist herself to the surface.

No, she shouldn't antagonise them on purpose to be left in the tunnels.

She should definitely not antagonise either of them.

For now.

Etta did the only thing she could think of.

She shut up and nodded.

The rest of the journey was shuffled in silence.

At the mole's door, the mouse gestured at Etta to start on her way back.

Etta stomped a few steps, then lowered the lantern and crept back to stand in the darkness behind the mole's door.

Maybe she'd overhear something useful.

She didn't even have to press her ear to the wooden door, sporting gaps the size of Etta's fist.

'No matter what SHE says, I'm not going to do it!' The mole's voice boomed. 'That girl is...is...well, you know how she is. Who would want to live with that?' He scoffed.

*Thanks...*Etta thought. *I find you equally unappealing.*

'When she says such horrible things, I cannot hear the sweet melody in her voice anymore. And it doesn't matter how pretty she is! I can't see her! I just won't do it, I won't do it!' The mole's protestations were getting more muffled.

Won't do what?

Come back to visit?

Fine by me!

'Is there anything I can do to persuade you?' She heard Missus Mouse say in a sultry voice.

'Why are you standing so close, Missus Mouse? What are you doing? Missus Mouse?' Mister Mole sounded shocked.

Something was flung at the door.

'Missus Mouse...your dress...ooh, your paws...your whiskers...ooh...' the mole now sounded doubtful.

'Oh, Missus Mouse...' drawled the lecherous mole.

Eeuw.

Etta almost made the sign of the cross like she had seen the old woman make many a time.

Instead, she ran all the way back, hoping the mouse-mole hanky-panky would last all night and she would have time to get her stash of food and maybe something for the make-shift rope.

If her dead friend wasn't going to fly her out of there, she could climb on top of it and with a make-shift rope hopefully climb out of the hole the mole had made.

***

Etta looked up.

The shimmering light of the stars above beckoned beyond her reach.

She climbed off her dead friend and eyed the swallow and the heap of linens next to it.

The gap between the bird and the hole in the tunnel ceiling was twice her size.

She had no chance of climbing out even if she managed to tie all the mouse's spare linens together.

She had nothing to hook the make-shift rope to even if by some miracle she would manage to twist the linen into a rope before the mouse returned.

Etta sighed and stuck her hands in her pockets.

Her right hand found her wand.

Her wonky wand.

That only parroted spells it was used to.

What use was a wand like that, even if the letter it came with had said to use the wand only in emergencies?

This was definitely an emergency!

And she had no useful spell to use!

She could go back and try again another night.

Except, she wouldn't put it past the mouse and the mole dismembering the bird and levelling the bits to make a new tunnel floor.

Or ordering her to do it!

They hadn't dared touch the bird when it was still breathing.

Now it was dead and in their way.

Etta eyed the wand thoughtfully.

What if?

The wand wouldn't probably do what she was about to tell it to do.

She knew one useless spell.

Might as well try it.

For this to really work, her wand should have been used to resurrect someone before.

Considering its restrictions were rather...menial...Etta figured there was a big chance this wouldn't work anyway.

Still, trying and failing was better than almost certain dismemberment.

Etta sighed, gripped her useless wand and tapped the bird on its chest three times. 'Resumo. Rescindo. Vitam ago.'

The bird twitched, its wing mended itself with a loud crack and before Etta could rejoice the swallow had darted out of the hole above it.

'No! Take me with you!' Etta shouted after it and hear a distant 'Tweet-tweet!'

Etta was left staring at a cloudy sky.

She sighed and looked at her wand.

The spell had worked.

Which could mean only one thing...

Someone had used THIS to bring someone back from the dead.

'What are you still doing here!' the mouse asked and Etta nearly jumped a mile.

How had the critter managed to sneak up on her in complete darkness?

The mouse glanced at Etta's wand, 'I asked you, girl, what are you doing here?'

Apparently, mouse-mole hanky-panky didn't last long or Etta had completely misunderstood what had gone on in there.

Or the Missus had run all the way back, which judging by her panting she might have.

Etta put her hands on her hips, trying to look fierce while she frantically thought how much time had passed since the mouse had shooed her off. 'I was walking! And...and... stargazing,' she said, glad her bag of supplies was hardly visible next to the wall where she had dropped it.

'I don't care what you were doing or why, you should have been home long ago and that's where we're going!' the mouse said and clutched Etta's arm. Her landlady's iron grip somewhat surprised Etta.

As the mouse practically dragged her back to whence Etta thought she had escaped, Etta couldn't help but think *Oh, well, at least the bird was free, if not entirely alive.*

Chapter 31. Marriage?!?!

As soon as they were back, the mouse locked the tunnel door and pocketed the key.

Etta was sorry she hadn't used every object in the mouse's household to heave on top of the bird to climb out instead of worrying about what the duo would do to the corpse.

She wasn't entirely sure she had done the swallow a service by bringing it back from the dead.

'We shall have a wedding,' Missus Mouse said, holding her hand to her heart.

'Congratulations!' Etta said and tried to look cheerful.

That was fast!

'What are you congratulating me for?' the mouse asked.

'You and Mister Mole...' Etta said, finding it strange that she had to spell it out.

'Don't be daft! *You* and Mister Mole, girl. You are the one he's supposed to wed,' the mouse explained.

'Supposed to by whom?' Etta demanded. 'And what makes you think I'd take your sloppy seconds?' she asked.

Finally, the old woman's romance section came in handy!

Either the mouse didn't understand her or she pretended not to hear. 'We shall have a small wedding, right here, in my home.' The Missus went into the kitchen and headed straight for the stove and Etta's secret stash of belladonna.

The mouse pulled out her flower pot and said, 'Even though it's winter, you shall have a bouquet. It's a good thing you've kept these alive. They will have to do.'

Etta's mouth fell open.

'Look how kind I am after everything you put me through...'

After everything I put YOU through?!?

The mouse prattled on, 'I mean, a girl should have flowers at least on her wedding day, if you will never have them during marriage...'

'Marriage? Are you out of your mind? We're two different species for a start!' Etta said and threw up her hands.

'I don't see how that is of any importance,' Missus Mouse huffed.

'Well, you wouldn't, would you, living celibate after husband dearest kicked the bucket,' Etta said and looked pointedly at the mouse whose snout went very pink very fast. 'And if that wasn't a deal-breaker, he lives way down below and I need light, I need the sun and the sky and the flowers, the fields...' she said.

'Yes, you'll have to forget about all those. HE dislikes them immensely - as you very well know!' The mouse said and looked at Etta reproachfully.

'Well, I don't!' Etta said. 'Whatever made both of you think I'd say yes? I've never given that mole any indication I even liked him!' Etta said.

'It's Mister Mole to you, girl! You sang to him and told him stories. Very crazy stories...'

'Not crazy, I told you, they all happened..' Etta protested.

'Crazy made-up stories, but it's your good luck that Mister Mole has a very hearty sense of humour,' Missus Mouse admonished.

'I sang while I was doing my chores. And I told YOU the stories because you asked me to tell them to you again. He just happened to be visiting,' Etta said.

The mouse smiled slyly.

'You did that on purpose?' She asked. 'It doesn't matter!' Etta shook her head. 'I'm not marrying him and that's final!' She spat and saw the mouse tug on the door handle and nod.

'You leave me no choice,' the mouse said and wriggled her whiskers. 'You ARE marrying Mister Mole and THAT's final!' The mouse said resolutely and patted her pocket.

'Oh, so you think you're going to keep me prisoner until I say yes?' Etta asked.

Seeing Etta reach for her pocket the mouse said, 'If you even think about using your wand - yes, I know about the wand, dear - then know this - I will bite off your wand hand, clean as a cleaver before you can cast any spell. I doubt that you know any, anyway. Spells, that is,' she added tartly.

Etta smoothed out her apron pocket and bit her lip.

The mouse's assumption wasn't strictly true, but she did have a wonky wand. Etta's wand didn't know any spells besides the useless household ones.

Those and raising the dead.

The mouse, sadly, was very much alive.

That could be rectified, though.

Just a few more drops than usual...

The mouse walked back to the stove, reached up and took one of the vases she never used.

Etta's heart sank.

The mouse pulled out Etta's stash of the nightshade drops. 'As lovely as your teas have been and as much as my restful nights may have helped decrease my...episodes...I'm not going to drink any tea anymore. With or without these,' the mouse poured the liquid down the sink.

There go my restful nights, Etta thought.

But hang on, not to miss the big picture here - the mouse knew about the wand! If she knew about the wand and the drops and the swallow...

Had the mouse herself left the wand with that letter for Daisy and then for Etta to find all along?

Out loud, Etta said 'Wand hand, huh?' And watched the mouse wriggle her whiskers, which she always did when annoyed or uncomfortable.

Well, at least she got some useful information as a side-dish to the involuntary incarceration. If normal wands worked when you held them in the hand you did most things with and her wand was rigged, then maybe she should try the spells with her non-dominant hand instead.

Etta plopped herself into one of Missus Mouse's armchairs and hung her feet over the arm rest. 'Since I now consider myself your unwilling prisoner and not a paying guest, don't expect me to cook and clean!' Etta said.

She'd figure out how to escape, eventually. She just needed to not be too tired to be able to run away.

'If you want to eat, you'll cook. Cleaning - I expect they'll be sending some new girl along soon enough,' Missus Mouse said.

'I wouldn't bet on it,' Etta said darkly.

Why would whoever was sending fairies this way send yet another when Etta was still here?

What if whoever was sending the fairies had run out of fairies to send?

What if whoever had taken Mister Mouse and possibly Daisy would be coming for Etta next?

The mouse paused for a moment, her whiskers twitching and paws doing hand-washing movements, which she only did when truly vexed.

'You're not about to have one of your episodes now, are you?' Etta asked and the mouse huffed.

'Remember what I told you about Mister Mole's quarters being grander and larger and much nicer than mine?' the mouse finally said with a kind smile and Etta nodded.

What did that have to do with anything? She'd have lots of room to run away from the gropey mole if she didn't manage to escape?

'Well, dear...I lied! It's a horrible dump! You've seen the way he behaves when he's here. How much cleaning do you think a blind mole can do all by himself?' The mouse squeaked and turned to go. 'I expect breakfast in the morning,' she threw over her shoulder without looking back.

'You can expect all you want, I'll only cook my share and none for you,' Etta said, meaning it.

***

Next evening, Etta still refused to lift a finger. She sat in the arm chair next to her would-be groom, ate stale cupcakes she had uncovered from the stash under her bed and watched the mouse scurry back and forth between the living room and the kitchen.

The mouse didn't look happy.

Good.

Tit for tat, as the old woman would say.

You incarcerate me - I stop being nice.

Like cooking and cleaning and telling stories or even having pleasant conversation or being civil.

Etta's prospective groom didn't mention the subject of marriage even once, so she was starting to think the mouse had made it all up to spite her last night.

In which case she was doubly satisfied at having exchanged their roles for the evening.

All of a sudden, there was quiet.

Too quiet.

The mouse was nowhere to be seen.

Etta pulled herself up and went to check on her landlady.

The mouse lay on her side on the dirty kitchen floor.

She had just...keeled over?

For a second, Etta panicked.

If the mouse were gone, what would the mole do to her?

Etta picked up a small pocket mirror from the window-sill and brought it to the mouse's whiskers.

The mirror misted over.

Phew!

'What's that you're doing in the kitchen, the both of you! Come, ladies, do keep me company! I would expect my bride to know her place...' the mole complained from the living room.

There go my high hopes that the mouse had made it all up, Etta thought.

Etta hunched over the mouse, 'Come now, let's get you to bed,' she said, taking her paw and raising the creature to her feet.

'I'll...do...no...such...thing...' the mouse whispered and leaned on Etta, trusting to be dragged into the living room.

'Oh, Mister Mole, I'm terribly sorry... I'm just... I'm just...'

'She fell over. Too tired from serving you all evening, I guess,' Etta said.

The mole huffed, 'Well, I never! You should have said... I should go...'

Etta watched the mouse.

If she was exhausted, would she...?

'Come on, girl,' the mouse said wincing and started for the door.

Either the mouse had no self-preservation skills or there was a good reason why she had to keep up with the stupid ritual of walking her guest back whence he came.

Or they didn't want to leave me alone.

The shuffle to the mole's abode took them forever.

Etta couldn't bring herself to think of it as her future home.

Ugh.

Most of the time, the mouse leaned heavily on the mole.

From his puffing, Etta gathered he was peeved.

They stopped just where the swallow had lain.

Etta's pulse quickened.

The mole offered the mouse his cane and she accepted.

The shuffle onward was as laborious as before.

Things were...

Awfully.

Mind-numbingly.

Boring.

Etta decided to spice things up a bit.

'Nobody noticed that the bird's gone? Seriously?' Etta asked pointing back with the lantern.

There was a pause and then the mole said, 'What's that you were saying?'

Exactly what he had said yesterday.

Not quite at the same spot, but spots were difficult to pin down in the dark.

'You come this way EVERY DAY. And for a week there was this huge bird lying here. So huge that you had a hard time squeezing past. It was dead yesterday. Now it's gone and you say you didn't notice?' Etta asked.

'Bird? What bird?' The mole asked, sounding alarmed.

'Pay her no attention, Mister Mole. As you know, the girl has a vivid imagination,' the mouse said and patted his arm.

Etta had a strong sense of deja-vu.

No matter what Etta said, the mouse and the mole were repeating the same dialogue from yesterday like a broken record as if...as if...this was a repeat performance like a play or something or like they were wound up to say certain things in certain places about certain other things.

Yesterday, she had provoked them.

Well, if they were repeating things, she could, too.

'What bird... A dead one! I came into the tunnels last night...all by myself...and dissected the bird with your chef's knife, Missus Mouse...' when Etta heard a gasp she smiled, 'oh, don't worry, I cleaned it afterwards...as I was saying, I chopped it into tiny little bits and carried them to the surface in your kitchen apron...' hearing another gasp, Etta reassured, 'don't worry, I washed that, too...and up top I scattered the poor creature...well, bits of it, to the wind. That's why you can move so freely through the passage today,' she finished, still smiling.

Etta saw the mole's back stiffen. His pace quickened.

The rest of the journey was a much quicker shuffle.

At the mole's door, the mouse disentangled herself from the mole and dropped her wretched self onto Etta, who didn't mind.

A mouse latching on to you was easier to control than a mouse scurrying off up ahead.

There were more ways than one to get the mouse to drop off into a dreamless sleep. Stopping under the hole on the way back - to get some fresh air - lots of fresh air after a hard day of work and a long walk - would undoubtedly help.

Chapter 32. The Dowry

Etta was watching the spindle.

That's right.

The spindle.

The bloody mouse had probably left all her other keys with the bloody mole to keep safe.

Etta wouldn't put it past the mouse to swallow the tunnel key just to spite her.

As much as Etta wished to climb out of the hole to the surface, wishing was all she had left at the moment.

There was no escaping the mouse.

Or the mole.

For now.

Come morning, the mouse had given her a spindle.

'What am I to do with that?' Etta asked, poking the thing with her finger.

'Why, to create your dowry, of course!' the mouse said.

'I have a perfectly good dress, why do I need to make more dresses?' Etta asked.

'The dress you have on is the only one you have,' the mouse stepped up to Etta and took her by the sleeve, 'And it's a bit fraying, don't you think?' The mouse pulled and Etta heard a rip. 'Wouldn't you rather look festive on your big day?' The mouse asked tartly.

'Not particularly. Even if you did do that on purpose. Hell will freeze over before I wed the mole,' Etta said and tried to adjust the sleeve back.

It was hopeless.

Etta ripped her other sleeve off as well.

'You will wed Mister Mole and it will be a lovely wedding. Just like mine!' the mouse snapped.

'Oh, right. I forgot you had a wedding you must have planned,' Etta said.

In half an hour.

The mouse's back straightened, 'Yes, I did. And *I* had a dowry, so you'll make one, too.'

If you met him one day and were married the next, you probably didn't make your own dowry, you wouldn't have had the time, Etta thought, but didn't say anything. *Maybe the mouse had prepared everything in anticipation.*

If the old woman had a wedding dress in her closet, why couldn't a mouse be as prepared?

'If you don't want to go around in rags, you'll make yourself new things to wear,' the mouse ordered.

'Why? He's blind. I might just as well run around naked, he won't be able to tell the difference,' Etta said, wanting to annoy the mouse just as much as she had vexed her.

The mouse hissed. 'How uncouth!'

'Speaking of uncouth - we have linen and cloth lying around, why don't you give me those and I can sew a dress or two much quicker than with this contraption,' Etta pointed at the wheel.

The mouse disappeared into her room.

She had finally managed to talk some sense into her!

When the mouse emerged with scissors in her paw and scraps of fluff on her snout, Etta blinked.

Her heart sank.

'Now that we don't have any linen or cloth lying around you will use that contraption to make at least your wedding dress and one more, for domestic purposes,' the mouse declared, dumping light-blue yarn into Etta's lap.

You'd better hide those scissors, sister, Etta thought.

Her face must have transmitted her thoughts as the mouse squealed, scampered and hid.

'The only reason I'm trying you to get to make a few dresses over a longer period of time is out of kindness, girl,' the mouse squeaked from behind the armchair. 'He doesn't have any light at his house. None at all. It hurts his eyes. That's why he has those dark glasses on when he's here and makes me dim all the lights and draw all the curtains. You won't have any light to sow or mend or spin soon. I thought you would like if it took you longer to make a nice dress or two, which could last you until spring and then you could perhaps come and visit me again and make another dress...' the critter's voice trailed off.

And here I thought you were trying to get me to use the spindle because it would keep me occupied and tire me out so I wouldn't have the energy to try anything stupid.

Like escape.

Facing pitch black with the mole did not appeal, with or without a new dress.

Wait....until spring? She was going to be living with the mole all the time until spring?!?

Etta shuddered.

Spring basically meant forever.

Ugh.

She had to get out of there!

Maybe, if she kept to herself and pretended to be spinning, the mouse would leave her alone enough for her to conjure up how to escape through that hole.

'Fine. I'll spin. A dress or two. But only if you leave me alone. I'll be in my room,' Etta said and hoisted the spinning wheel onto her back.

Where the mouse had dug this one up, was a mystery.

Maybe it had been delivered?

Maybe the mole had had it all along?

Although Etta couldn't lock her door, the mouse stayed out of her room for most of the day. Only once did she pop her head in to ask whether dinner was forthcoming.

Etta threw a pillow at her head and yelled, 'I'm not hungry, you go nibble on some cheese!'

The Missus disappeared to her room and didn't bother Etta anymore.

The mouse was lucky that the spinning wheel was too heavy to throw.

Etta thought she heard a creak.

The tunnel door.

Etta went to check it out.

The tunnel door was locked.

The mouse was nowhere to be seen.

If she had left, she had probably taken the key along.

Ever since the mouse had threatened Etta with marriage she had kept all the keys somewhere where Etta couldn't find them.

Probably at the mole's.

The tunnel key the mouse kept under her cap during the day and under her pillow at night.

Etta wouldn't put it past the mouse to swallow the tunnel key just to spite her.

As much as Etta wished to climb out of the hole to the surface, wishing was all she had left at the moment.

There was no escaping the mouse.

Or the mole.

For now.

Oh, well.

On the other hand...

She could make herself something to eat!

When she opened the pantry cupboard she found it empty.

So was the next cupboard.

Etta searched the entire kitchen.

There were only dirty dishes and nothing else.

Not even a dried onion.

Not even a mouldy turnip.

The mouse had taken every edible thing with her to the mole's?!?

Etta went to check on her stash and found that pillaged too.

How?

When?

When Etta had slept?

She had to get out of here!
Etta's stomach grumbled.
'I'm sorry. I have nothing to cook,' she apologised to her insides.
Her insides grumbled again.
Etta took one last look around the kitchen.
Not a scrap of food.
Well...that was...spiteful.
Even if the mouse had packed everything edible up and just left it outside of the tunnel door, Etta was still on the wrong side of the door.
Etta tried to remember if she had done any food spells with Caroline.
Caroline had had the scones ready before Etta got there.
The tea Etta had made herself.
Nope, no food spells.
Etta sighed and boiled some water.
Tea it was.
Again.
Back in her room, with a tea-cup in hand, Etta sighed again, looked at the spinning wheel and kicked at the fluff on the floor.
Soon, all that fluff from the wool would be gathering into dust-bunnies.
She'd be damned if she was going to do any cleaning, the mouse can see to it herself!
Looking at the woollen fluff billowing off the floor Etta tried to remember the spell to make tiny bits of fibres assemble into a small cloth rectangle.
It was the first spell she had tried with her own wand and succeeded.
Maybe if she tried only part of the spell...
'*Convenio linteum!*' she said pointing at the yarn on the spindle. The wand emitted a few sparks and then all the yarn disassembled itself into fluff and all the fluff assembled itself into a sky-blue linen cloth.

Well, whaddaya know...dropping the rectangle part worked!

There was probably a different spell to tell the cloth to assemble into a dress.

Too bad they hadn't tried that one.

Still, out of this cloth she could now sew a dress much faster. She could even have a dress by tonight, if the mouse kept away for a few hours.

She'd hide it, of course.

Under or inside her covers since it was safe to assume the mouse knew about all her secret stashes.

She needed to replenish the wheel, though.

Etta wandered over to the mouse's room and opened her cupboards one after another.

What she found left her speechless.

She could definitely get her spinning wheel replenished.

Blue, white, pink, yellow.

Yarn, yarn and more yarn.

In all of the cupboards.

How many dresses did the mouse expect her to make?

Those critters better not expect me to make their festive clothes as well, Etta thought.

She selected two heaps, one light-blue and another pitch black, fluffing the remainder so as to conceal the dent she'd made in the mouse's reserves.

When she had restocked the wheel, she lay out the light-blue fabric on her bed.

She would need clothes for the cold trek out of here. But before she got to do that, first and foremost, she needed to make a rope to climb out. How she would attach it to something up top was beyond her at the moment, but she would think of that later.

It would be such a shame to waste this light-blue cloth on a rope, though.

Etta went back to the mouse's cupboard and retrieved the dullest yarn she could find.

Better.

She told it to assemble and it did.

Then she told the black yarn to assemble and it did.

Out of the black cloth Etta sewed a hooded cloak and hid it inside her duvet cover.

Not too festive, but better for hiding in the tunnels.

A double-layered light-blue dress was next.

Sewing, Etta couldn't help but think of the dowry the mouse expected her to make and marriage in general. She remembered the tale the old woman used to read to her of two lovers who both ended up dead, one by poison the other by dagger. Rather soon after the marriage had been consummated.

She shuddered at the thought.

How was copulation with a mole going to look like?

No, no, no, no, no.

No, thank you!

She'd rather take poison!

She would prefer an anti-love-potion for the mole, to be honest.

Too bad it was winter or she could experiment with wild flowers and herbs.

If that girl Juliet had used an anti-love potion on her suitor Paris or even on that Romeo, Etta bet that the boys would have left her the heck alone and maybe nobody would be dead.

Etta wished the mouse and the mole would leave her the heck alone.

Then she wouldn't need to think about poisoning herself or anyone else for that matter.

She sighed.

I can thank Daisy for all of this!

If something hadn't happened to Daisy, she would still be here and she'd be the one making the dowry and preparing for an inter-species wedding and I'd still be free to frolic around in the woods.

Or living with the undead.

Living with the undead sounded pretty good by comparison to what the mouse expected her to do.

Maybe the mouse had also offered Daisy to the mole and Daisy had said no?

Maybe that's why they got rid of her?

Remembering the mouse's and mole's cavalier attitude towards dead things and the mouse's threats to leave Etta in the tunnels, Etta shuddered.

No, no, no, no, no.

She had seen no bones in the tunnel.

No, no, no, no, no!

Daisy MUST be alive somewhere, just like Caroline.

She had to be!

I hope not exactly like Caroline, even if she was alive-ish, living in a fairy-tale.

Maybe Daisy was in another fairy-tale?

While Etta was being made to marry inter-species against her will...

Hang on...

Was SHE in a fairy-tale and didn't know it?

A defenceless girl being forced to marry an ugly mole by a turncoat mouse who had offered lodgings and then locked the girl up definitely had a ring of a fairy-tale about it.

Etta looked at the spindle and tried to remember all fairy-tales with spindles in them.

The Sleeping Beauty?

Nope, Etta and everyone around her was very much awake.

But if some weird gnome was going to appear and offer to help in exchange for her firstborn, at least she knew what to call him.

Rumpelstiltskin!

Bring it on!

Etta stared at the door.

No-one came.

Oh, well.

Etta remembered that in some of the fairy-tales the old woman used to read to her the heroes and heroines were tested.

Maybe this marriage to the mole was a test?

Of what? Saying no to the wrong guy?

Hang on, the toad...the toad had also wanted her to marry her ugly son.

There was a definite theme here.

Marriage.

And come to think of themes....

The toad had considered her beautiful.

Her second kidnapper, the cockchafer whom all the other cockchafers had called odd and shamed him into letting her go...he had also thought she was beautiful, though she had been called ugly by his kin.

Beauty.

Maybe vanity was also an issue?

Etta had no idea how she felt about either marriage or vanity. She hadn't thought about them for the first fifteen years of her life and didn't see why she should start now.

Etta heard the rustle of a key in the tunnel door.

She quickly hid the half-finished dress under her bed covers and pretended to be spinning the yarn as the mouse walked in.

'Well, you haven't even made a dent, have you?' the mouse said disapprovingly.

More than you know.

'I helped you to stall, not avoid the inevitable,' the mouse said.

'I'm afraid I'm not familiar with the contraption and I'm doing as best as I can...under the circumstances,' Etta said.

The mouse nodded, 'Well, don't look at me, I don't know how to spin either. It'll probably take you a few weeks to get the two dresses done...well, we can have the wedding in a couple of weeks then...' she shrugged.

Yes, now that you think you have me locked up and starving and spinning wildly all day, you think you have all the time in the world, Etta thought and tried not to look gleeful.

18. 'Why, now! And instant success!' Caroline beamed.

Chapter 33. Guests and Godmothers

Having double checked that the mouse was sleeping soundly, Etta took out her half-finished dress, sat on the edge of her bed and imagined Caroline was there.

What she wouldn't give to see Caroline's friendly face this very minute!

Caroline's decaying, bossy, friendly face!

A poof and a stinky skirmish later, a certain undead person gathered her limbs up from Etta's floor.

'Hello! You called?' Caroline said and Etta almost squealed in delight.

Instead she joyfully hissed 'Caroline! How? I mean why... I mean how are you here?'

Etta darted out of her room to check that Caroline's arrival hadn't woken the mouse.

The mouse was fast asleep and snoring loudly.

'I found a rather interesting spell to let me know when someone wants to see me and here I am!' The corpse bride beamed, throwing back what remained of her black mane.

'Wow! Caroline...that was...that was inspired!' Etta commended, setting the dress down on the spinning wheel.

'I was wondering what had happened to you when you didn't show up for tea and cakes a week ago, like we agreed,' Caroline whispered.

Cakes!

Etta perked up, 'You don't happen to have any cakes with you right now, do you?' she asked.

Caroline nodded and produced a dried scone which Etta scoffed down in one go.

'Wow!' was all Caroline said, catching her falling eye mid-goggle. 'Oops... 'You were supposed to go check on the mouse and come straight back. What happened?' Caroline added quickly, shifting the attention back to Etta. 'Did something bad happen to the mouse and you needed to stay longer than you planned?'

'That's for sure,' Etta muttered. 'Why didn't you use the *Excio Etta* spell to check on me?'

'I know I have it written down, but I forgot the pronunciation again...' Caroline looked sheepish.

Oh, for the love of all that was sacred!

'I will write the pronunciation down for you,' Etta promised.

'So, when pronunciation got the best of me...I mean, the wand can't pronounce things, so...I searched for a spell that would alert me when you thought of me or wanted to see me,' Caroline beamed.

'I did think of you!' Etta said, suddenly feeling ashamed she hadn't thought of Caroline at all after the mouse had sprung marriage on her.

Had Caroline been trying and trying and trying and Etta wasn't...?

'When did you come up with that spell?' she asked Caroline.

'Why, now! And instant success!!' Caroline beamed.

Etta exhaled in relief. 'And now you're here!!! Boy, am I glad you're here!!' she said.

'Yes, yes, I am!' Caroline nodded, her eyes rolling around in her eye sockets.

Etta wanted to hug her, but the stench was so prohibitive she desisted.

'I smell even worse now, don't I?' Caroline asked sadly and sat on the edge of Etta's bed.

Great! Now she'd need to wash the bed linen before she could sleep in there.

Out loud Etta said, 'So what? Personally, I think you're great! Especially for coming to rescue me.'

'I know,' Caroline said and sniffled. 'But I smell really really badly now and I'm really really worried.'

Etta tried to smile. 'I've missed you,' she said. *Warts and all. Like focusing on her stink instead of on my rescue.*

Caroline looked at her reproachfully.

'Ok, so you stink,' Etta shrugged.

'I didn't know the Enchantress I agreed to become would end up a stinky Enchantress,' Caroline pouted.

'Darling, I don't think the queen thought it through or perhaps she didn't know,' Etta said.

'The queen? What does she have to do with me stinking?' Caroline asked.

'Everything,' Etta said and sidled up to Caroline.

'Why?' the fairy asked.

'I did tell you the first time we met, but you didn't believe me and later I didn't know how to tell you so that you would believe me...' Etta said.

Caroline sniffled, 'Maybe I didn't want to believe. Maybe you didn't explain well enough. Maybe I wanted to believe everything would be ok. Maybe...'

'You're babbling,' Etta pointed out.

'Oh, I know, but it's hard...admitting out loud that I'm...I'm...' she exhaled and said, '...that I am the walking dead...' her voice faded into the tiniest of whispers.

'I am, aren't I?' she asked.

Etta nodded. 'I'm afraid so. But at least you're not repeating one day over and over again.'

Caroline sniffled again.

'Tell me, is the Beast a Beast all the time now? Did the spell work?' Etta asked.

Caroline stopped sniffling and nodded, 'It did. I had to wait around for a couple of days to make sure. He didn't change back. Boy, was he not pleased. I barely escaped his castle in one piece!'

'And?'

Caroline looked surprised, 'And...I was free!'

'So, where did you go? What did you do?' Etta asked.

'Everywhere!' Caroline said. 'There was a village and a girl and... I was able to go and see places and do things that I wanted to do,' she said as her eyes glistened. 'Although people fled from me, shrieking and kept calling me Frankie Stein.'

'Frankenstein,' Etta corrected her.

'Bless you!' Caroline said. 'Do you need a handkerchief?' she asked and pulled a white dainty thing from her pocket along with a billow of dust. 'Talk about a case of mistaken identity.'

Etta nodded slowly, but had to agree with the villagers.

Caroline in advanced stages of decay looked pretty scary.

'So, tying the Beast to that,' Caroline coughed, 'rose was,' another cough, 'a gift,' she was caught in a coughing fit. When she looked down at what she had coughed out it turned out to be a tooth. 'Oh, no... Look, my decay is accelerating...'

Etta tried not to look horrified. She wanted to hug Caroline, but was afraid she might fall to pieces if she did.

They sat in silence for a while.

Finally Etta decided to brave it.

If she had to wash the bed linen anyway, what was another dress between friends?

She hazarded a hug.

Please don't fall apart, please don't fall apart, please don't fall apart, Etta thought as she embraced the skin and bones that was Caroline.

Caroline didn't fall apart.

'How long do you think I've got?' Caroline asked quietly into Etta's shoulder.

Etta disentangled herself and looked straight into Caroline's faded baby blues, 'Oh, honey, I really don't know. We can check the spell-book to see if it says anything, if you want? Only, I'd need your help in getting away from here to yours...'

'No need,' Caroline beamed and produced the book from under her cloak, 'I brought it with me. Just in case you needed help with something, you know.'

Etta hugged her again.

What's a few bed linen and a dress and a long, long, long shower between friends?

'Caroline, you're a star!' Etta took the book, 'Now let's find out, shall we?'

Half an hour later they were both miserable.

'If the resurrected only keep for a year before they completely disintegrate, then I only have a month or two at most...' Caroline whispered. 'This sucks.'

'Let's focus on the positive here,' Etta said.

'On the positive? How about: I'm positive this sucks!' Caroline exclaimed and Etta shushed her, rushing to check on the mouse.

The mouse was still out cold.

Who knew the exercise from doing her own chores meant the mouse was as good as dead to the world.

Had I known that, I could have done without doing her chores and without drugging her!

'Let's focus on what it is that you'd like to do during the time that you have left.' Etta said, carefully avoiding any reference to the amount of time that was Caroline's life expectancy.

Or was it death expectancy?

'Like, what do you want to do right now?' Etta asked, trying to look bright as day.

'I'd like to try on one of your dresses,' Caroline said and turned her nose up. 'This one,' she pointed at the light-blue one hanging on the wheel.

'It's not finished yet,' Etta said.

'Then by all means - finish it!' Caroline suggested.

Etta smiled mischievously and rummaged around in the spell-book, then snatched away Caroline's wand, 'I'll borrow that, thank you!'

'*Finio vestis!*' Etta said and saw a dress assemble itself.

'It's yours!' Etta said and helped Caroline into it, making sure the minimal amount of skin fell off and no bones stuck out where they shouldn't. 'There! You look gorgeous!'

'I do, don't I?' Caroline said, sniffling. She twirled and to Etta's horror a faint cover of dust ebbed from Caroline and hung in the air, settling everywhere around them.

Great! No sleeping tonight until she had scrubbed her bedroom top to bottom.

The mouse was going to get her wish.

At least where one room was concerned.

'You borrowed my wand. Yours still doesn't work, I presume?' Caroline asked and Etta nodded.

'Do you want me to disenchant your wand?' Caroline reached for the spell-book.

Etta's mouth dropped open, 'Wow! *Quid pro quo*, Caroline, really? Yes, please!' Etta said so loudly Caroline had to shush her.

'I wouldn't mind an unlocking spell either,' Etta whispered and thought this was an opportune time to tell Caroline about how the mouse had imprisoned her and why.

Caroline shook her head, 'She shouldn't have done that.'

'If only my wand had worked, I wouldn't be stuck here!' Etta whispered.

'Do you know what's wrong with it?' Caroline asked.

'It just does spells it has done before, but no new spells.' Etta said.

'That's interesting,' Caroline said.

'Annoying is what it is,' Etta retorted.

'Give me your wand!'

Etta did.

Caroline took it very gently, like a wounded animal. 'Now I have to be careful that the wand doesn't turn back into whatever or whomever it used to be before it was shaped into a wand.'

Wands used to be things or beings and were shaped into wands?

'Now, you just need it to do spells, like mine does, right? So we need to remove the restriction to do new spells, right?' Caroline asked Etta who nodded.

'*Baculum magicum: omnia fac similiter!*' Caroline said and pointed her wand at Etta's wand.

'That's it? You told my wand to do all enchantments?' Etta asked and Caroline nodded.

'Try it!'

'Where's that unlocking spell,' Etta asked and eyed the book.

Caroline let her leaf through it.

'Found it!' Etta said.

They had definitely not done this one before. And it was so simple, too!

'Aperio!' Etta told to the front door and pointed her wand at the key hole.

She heard a satisfying click.

Who needs a key when you have fairy friends.

Who can break and enter at will at all hours of the night and fix your wands and teach you spells.

It was good to have friends. Which reminded her.

Etta took a piece of paper, 'Here, let me write down the pronunciation of the *Excio* spell for you - eks-ski-o or x ski and o like door, not o like do. Got it?'

Caroline nodded.

'I want to try it with my own wand, just in case,' Etta said.

'But I'm already here! ' Caroline said.

'There's another fairy I've been meaning to introduce to you...' Etta started.

'Really? There are more fairies here besides you and me?' Caroline said with a twinge of something in her voice. 'So, you won't miss me at all when I'm gone, will you?' she sniffled.

'I will miss you, it's just that I don't know what happened to the fairy who stayed with the mouse before me. She just... disappeared. Maybe the mouse and the mole did something horrid to her. I just want to find her to make sure she's alive!' Etta said.

Caroline pretended to think for a moment, but Etta saw her 'alive' comment had struck a chord. 'Very well, who are we looking for?' Caroline asked.

'Daisy. Her name is Daisy,' Etta said and raised her wand. '*Excio Daisy!*' Etta demanded from her newly repaired wand.

The air beside the bed wobbled and through a rectangle that reminded Etta of the old woman's television they could see Daisy sweeping up a kitchen and talking to a girl in ratty clothes who was polishing the cooking pot.

A portal!

'Ooh, a magic mirror!' Caroline said.

Daisy looked up, raised her sooty arm to her eyes and asked, 'Etta, is that you?'

Etta waved and sidled closer to the 'magic mirror'. 'Hey, Daisy! Long time, no see. How have you been? We thought we'd have a bit of a chat. Are you free?' She asked, all in one go.

'We?' Daisy squinted.

Caroline waved at her.

'Oh, my...' was all Daisy said and Etta gave wordless thanks for her politess. 'Well, Ella is up to her eyeballs here...'

Someone behind Daisy hissed, 'Would you just go! Geesh! I would pay you to go away and leave me be for five minutes, if I had any money...' said a sooty, vaguely female-looking creature in rags and added, pointing at the portal, 'which I don't, so don't get your hopes up, but do take my lovely fairy godmother off my hands for at least...an hour. I could do with an hour of rest from 'Ella, clean this!' and 'Ella, fetch that!' and 'Ella, sit up straight or you'll never marry the prince!" The girl made a face and muttered 'As if that's ever going to happen...'

Daisy pouted, 'Cynthia Eleanor Alyxandra Monfort! You do know I'm doing this for your own good! That's what fairy godmothers are for!' she said, fluttering her wings.

To Etta and Caroline Daisy said, 'Please meet my charge, Cinderella, a future princess, currently in training,' she added hesitantly, seeing Ella wipe her nose on her sleeve.

'Charmed,' Etta said and Caroline waived.

'Well, I'd wish you'd do a lot more magicking and a lot less mothering, truth be told...' the girl admitted and Daisy rolled her eyes, absent-mindedly lifting a muffin to her mouth.

'Give me that!' Etta said and grabbed for the muffin, expecting to catch air.

Her hand went through the portal.

Next thing she knew, her fingers had closed around the muffin.

'Your hand,' Caroline peeked behind the mirror, 'I can see only half of it! Up until your wrist!'

'The other half is in my face,' Daisy said helpfully.

Etta yanked her hand back.

Together with the blueberry muffin.

'Oi, give it back!' Daisy said and reached out.

Etta slapped at Daisy's fingers which had crossed over into her bedroom. 'Get a new one! I haven't had food all day today, the bloody mouse hid all the supplies, probably wants to starve me into submission, so have some compassion,' Etta said through the bites, scoffing down the last crumbs and licking her fingers. 'Got any more?' she asked, craning her neck into Daisy's kitchen.

Daisy nodded, 'Sure, we have loads! Are you sure Missus Mouse didn't just forget?'

'Not we. It's not for us! It's for the gents and don't make me make even a sandwich for her, I can't, I'm too tired!' Ella hissed from behind Daisy.

'Long story,' Etta told Daisy. 'Come on over and I'll tell you all about it. Bring some of those muffins,' she added as Cinderella hissed.

Daisy looked sceptical. 'Are you sure the spell is stable?' she asked.

Etta shrugged. 'The port...erm...magic mirror is holding up well so far and my wand now works, so we can conjure up safe passage any time we want.'

'Your wand didn't work?' Daisy asked and Etta rolled her eyes.

'Just come on over already!' Etta said.

'Oh, very well,' Daisy said, stuck a loaf of bread under her arm, grabbed three apples and extended her hand through the portal. 'Help me across, please!'

Etta took Daisy's hand and pulled her through. The portal remained active, hovering next to Etta's bed and showing them Cinderella setting the table for one, looking a lot happier than before.

Daisy tested the magic mirror with her hand. From Cinderella's hiss they gathered it let her back through alright. 'Ok, this works both ways. Lovely!' Daisy said and Caroline nodded so vigorously her neck started creaking.

'Careful, dear,' said Daisy and extended her hand, 'Hello, I'm Daisy!'

'Caroline,' said Caroline and barely touched the proffered hand, which seemed to suit Daisy just fine as she smiled widely.

Etta gave Daisy points for not gagging over the smell.

Caroline and Daisy looked at each other, one with suspicion, the other with awe.

'I didn't realise there were more fairies besides Etta and me,' Daisy said. 'You are a fairy, right?'

'Not for much longer,' Caroline bit off and filled Daisy in on her predicament.

'Oh, how terrible, dear! How do you feel about it?' Daisy asked.

Caroline sniffled, 'Pretty horrible, actually. I'm really, really scared...' she whispered, casting glances at Etta who was tap-tapping her foot.

'Yes, but you have a plan how to make the most of it and time is precious,' Etta said and looked from Caroline to Daisy.

'Does either of you have an idea how not one but three fairies ended up in the enchanted wood where nobody but one mouse, one mole and one colony of May bugs live?'

Chapter 34. Fifteen, Sixteen, Seventeen

'I don't know the mouse and the mole, do you?' Caroline asked Daisy.

'Not the mole, him I never met, but I was the mouse's maid before Etta,' Daisy said. 'You?' she asked Caroline who shook her head.

'That's what I mean...' Etta said, 'We all have similar experiences but not quite and I, personally, would like to get to the bottom of this.'

Two pairs of eyes, brown and fading blue, were on her.

'What do you mean, similar experiences?' Caroline asked.

'When I met you, you had just...' *fallen to your death, jumped from the top of the oak tree...* 'met the May bugs, I believe?' Etta chose to be more diplomatic for the sake of a more fruitful discussion.

Caroline nodded.

'Well, I've met them too and didn't find them very charming,' Etta said and made a face.

'They were quite rude,' Daisy said and clapped her hand over her mouth. 'I didn't mean to be mean,' she said in a small voice.

'Daisy, it's ok. You're being truthful, not mean,' Etta said.

'So, we have all met the May bugs...' Caroline mused, 'The question is how?' She looked superior. 'I was rescued by one of them from a floating lily leaf. Goodness knows where that stupid butterfly would have dragged me otherwise...' she said.

'My butterfly's name was Annabel, she was and I hope still is a *Heliconius,* happily married and a mother of two,' Etta interjected, watching the faces of the other fairies drop, 'She refused to go in one specific direction, south, and was otherwise going round and round as if...as if...'

'She was waiting for the May bugs to come and pick you up...' Daisy finished for her. 'Yes, I got the same sense, now that you mention it...'

'Did we all get rescued by May bugs from lily leaves drawn by a butterfly?' Etta asked and got nods.

'Maybe it was the same bug or the same butterfly?' Daisy offered.

Etta and didn't have the heart to tell them about the graveyard.

Caroline looked thoughtful, 'My butterfly was pink, I think.'

'Yellow,' said Daisy.

'Blue,' said Etta and decided not to traumatise the girls with how many pink and yellow wing remnants she had burnt. 'So, we have three different butterflies...' Etta said. 'Annabel told me they are in the habit of helping stranded fairies in return for their gambling debts being erased.'

'Gambling debts erased? How? By whom?' Daisy asked and Etta filled them in, adding, 'By whom, I actually don't know. Neither did Annabel, I think. She said she got her orders on where to fly from the house of cards where she incurred her debt.'

'If the butterflies have a habit of helping stranded fairies, then they must have helped more than just the three of us,' Caroline said.

Thinking back to the graveyard Etta nodded, 'Yes, lots more.'

'How do you know?' Daisy and Caroline asked in unison.

Etta sighed and had to tell them about the butterfly graveyard.

'Oh, how terrible!' Daisy gushed as Caroline looked at Etta with reproach, 'Why didn't you tell me when you were visiting!'

Etta shrugged, 'You didn't ask me much about my world.'

'I see why you feel something fishy is going on. It's like we are in a repeating story of sorts.' Daisy said. 'And if there were lots of butterflies, where are all the fairies?'

'Not here. Just like you and Caroline are no longer in the enchanted part of the wood, but we'll get to that later.' Etta said. 'About the fishes...did you two meet them too?'

Both girls nodded.

They sat in silence.

'Did we go through things in the same sequence?' Etta asked.

'Before the May bugs was the butterfly...' Daisy said and Caroline and Etta nodded.

'Before the butterfly came the fishes who bit my lily leaf free from where it sat in the middle of the water...' said Caroline as the others nodded.

'And before then was the toad in the middle of the night and the ugly hag who kept me prisoner for as long as I can remember,' Daisy said and Caroline nodded.

'You, too?' Daisy asked and reached out to hug Caroline but getting a whiff of her, decided to pat her dress sleeve instead.

Etta shook her head. 'Before the butterfly and the fishes and the toad I lived with a nice old lady for as long as I can remember...' she said.

'With Caroline never meeting the mouse, this is the second discrepancy in an otherwise repetitive tale.' Etta said.

Daisy looked at the others, 'Maybe there is such a thing as a good discrepancy? How old are you? I'm fifteen.'

Etta said, 'I'm almost sixteen.'

'Seventeen,' said Caroline.

'That's what I mean! Finally a good discrepancy!' Daisy beamed.

Etta furrowed a brow and Caroline inclined her head, 'Why?'

'We are all fairies. Well, you don't have wings, dear,' she told Etta, 'but you're the only one who is still stuck in these woods and Caroline and I have earned our wings...'

'So?' Caroline asked.

'Don't you see? With such age differences, we might be related, don't you think?' Daisy swished her hair back and smiled, her baby-browns alight.

Etta looked at what remained of Caroline's ink black hair and then at Daisy's blond bob and said, 'I have red hair and green eyes. Caroline has black hair and blue eyes and Daisy, your eyes are brown and your hair is blond. As far as I know from genetics, the chances of any two of us being sisters and all three of us being related...the chances of that...for all I know, the chances of that might be astronomical...' Etta said.

'Gene-what? Astro-where?' Daisy asked.

Etta sighed. 'Let me explain. There are several ways we can figure out whether or not we are related. One is to take our blood and compare,' Etta pointed to the vein in her arm as Daisy *eeuwed* while Caroline put her arms behind her back, 'But we don't have the equipment to do this.' She saw the other fairies visibly relax. 'Another way is to think this through logically,' Etta said and the others nodded. 'Having been raised by my kind old woman, I don't actually know where I came from. I doubt you two do either?' The other fairies shook their heads. 'But we had to come from somewhere.' Nods all around. 'Like from the flower colonies from the flower fields the bug flew over on its way to the oak?'

'There are flower colonies?' Daisy gushed. 'Then maybe we gravitated towards each other's company because fairies live together, rather than alone...' Daisy said.

'Possibly,' Etta said and tapped her chin. 'Ok. Let's use assumptions and approximate and see where that gets us. Let's assume a fairy colony has a population of say, twenty thousand fairies,' Etta said and heard Daisy gasp.

'Let's say fairies live to be a hundred,' Etta said and heard Caroline gasp.

'Let's also assume there are fairies of all different ages, so age zero to one hundred in a population of twenty thousand. Let's assume couples and not polygamy. That's ten thousand couples. Fertile age is from roughly fifteen until say, sixty-five,' Etta said as Daisy put up her hand.

Etta patted Daisy's knee. 'These are just assumptions, ok? I don't know any of this for sure, same as you. But let's discard the population that is no longer breeding, the really young and the really old, that leaves us with about...five thousand couples.

Let's assume not everybody wants kids. And, judging by my old woman, not everybody who wants kids can actually have them. Let's see, shall we say two thousand couples with kids? And if we assume at least one child per couple, then that's roughly two thousand children. So, if one colony of twenty thousand fairies has about two thousand kids, then those kids...'

'...Are more likely to be related than not.' Caroline said. 'Are you saying that we could be related?'

Etta nodded slowly. 'If we are three out of those 2000 or less kids from one fairy colony, then we are likely to be related. Maybe distant cousins or something, but still...'

'If we ARE, indeed, all from one fairy colony,' Caroline said. 'Maybe there are colonies where fairies have black hair and blue eyes and maybe blond fairies live in another colony and redheads yet another,' Caroline said, pointing at Etta's mane. 'In which case we might be from different clans.'

'Yes!' Etta said. 'If there are less fairies than we assumed, then at some point inter-marriages would no longer produce healthy offspring and the fairies would either die out or have to find other fairies outside of their own colony to marry.'

'Like inter-clan marriages,' Daisy piped up.

'Looking at our physical differences, I can only assume mixing with other clans has already happened.' Etta said. 'Blonds usually have blue eyes and dark hair usually goes with brown eyes. Which doesn't mean we couldn't be related. We could try to analyse how closely we could be related, but...'

I don't really want to make all those calculations, Etta thought. The hair and eye genes were tricky. She had to do a lot of calculations before she could even hazard a guess. Besides, it didn't matter anyway. It wasn't like they were discussing reasons to avoid too close a marriage and breeding with too close relatives.

Out loud she said, 'We are already as good as sisters, don't you agree?'

Daisy squeezed Etta's hand, 'It doesn't matter if we are or aren't sisters or even relatives. One way or another, we are bound by an interestingly similar fate, it seems.'

'So we could be related or...not,' Caroline summed up, staring at Etta.

A silence settled, pierced only by the mouse's snores.

'I remember climbing to the rafters of the small house where the hag kept me and reaching a narrow dusty window to sneak a peek outside. There were only weeds and roofs and a huge house with glass windows, probably where the old hag lived herself,' Caroline reminisced.

'Me, too!' Daisy piped up.

'Ooh, did your evil hag have a long nose with a huge wart on the...'

'Left side!' Caroline and Daisy said in unison and Etta shushed them.

'Our evil hag,' Caroline stressed, 'had a bit of a hump?' she asked and Daisy nodded, 'Wore awfully stinky clothes...and... and she didn't talk much...?' Daisy asked.

Caroline nodded and added, 'Like speech was difficult for her or something.'

Etta inclined her head, remembering her kind old woman saying she's going outside for a cigarette, which always made her clothes smell peculiar. And while one of her shoulders had been higher than the other, Etta wouldn't exactly call it a hump. Like she wouldn't call a large freckle on the left side of the old woman's nose a wart.

'Once, I thought I saw a tiny fairy behind the window in that huge house and I remember I pitied the thing,' Caroline said and turned her sights on Etta.

'Yes, imagine, if she ignored us the way she did, what horrors befell that poor thing she singled out!' Daisy said and stopped abruptly, staring at Etta as well.

'It appears that the one living with the hag was the luckiest of us all,' Caroline said, her mouth twitching. 'The hag taught her how to read and write and taught her Latin and about... genetics and astronomy, was it?' Caroline spat as Etta nodded.

'How do you know?' Daisy asked.

'The person that you refer to as the evil hag I called mother for fifteen years,' Etta said, facing the facts.

'Mother?' Daisy's mouth formed an O.

'Mother,' Etta said.

'Are we all related to our evil captor?' Daisy looked distressed and Etta shook her head.

'I'm not related to the old woman...sorry, hag. She couldn't have any more children, but she wanted to care of someone. She got me from a witch and took me to live in that big house. I didn't have any choice. I didn't even know there were other fairies out there. I tried exploring the garden, but as soon as I asked about the sheds...the small houses, she forbade me to go outside,' Etta said.

'So you don't know why you had the privilege of living in the house?' Caroline asked.

'No,' Etta said and shook her head.

She really didn't.

Caroline looked thoughtful, 'Still, besides me never meeting the mouse, you being held up at the house is another discrepancy. I'm discounting the colours of butterflies.'

'Why not?' Daisy asked.

'Same function,' Caroline and Etta said in unison.

'It seems that all three of us have suffered the same fate, except for how we fared with the mouse...' Daisy said.

'Gilded cage or not, you were still held captive, Etta, and you were also still abducted, same as us,' Caroline pronounced.

Etta nodded slowly. In the space of these few nods her home had transformed into a prison.

The realisation of what had really happened was what made the difference.

'I still can't believe your evil hag was the same old woman who was kind to me,' Etta sighed.

'Kind? You call someone who forgets to feed you for a week kind?' Caroline huffed.

'She was kind to me,' Etta shrugged. 'I didn't know she kept other fairies in worse conditions nearby and hardly spoke to them. Considering how badly she treated you, both of you turned out very fine!' Etta said.

'How many of us do you think the hag, your old woman, kept there?' Daisy asked.

Etta tried to remember. 'There were at least ten sheds, I think.'

And to think, she had called that woman mother!

'Who would have done this? Kept fairies incarcerated? And why?' Daisy asked the most obvious of questions.

'I don't know. I doubt the old hag would have done it by herself. She wasn't the type. She actually loved children. She couldn't have any herself,' Etta tried to explain away the actions of her sometime mother.

'Well, keeping...was it ten sheds, you said?...keeping ten kids incarcerated for about fifteen years was a funny way of showing she loved us,' Caroline snorted, holding on to her nose just in case.

'I don't know why she treated me differently, maybe she ran out of sheds. I would have loved it, if both of you would have lived at the house! We could have been friends way back when!' Etta blurted out.

Instead of now when two of us were all but tied to our kitchens, so still incarcerated and now also in slavery while the third was dead and decaying.

'Friends?' Caroline asked.

Etta realised she'd have to explain the concept, so she did.

'I met you first, so we were friends first!' cried Caroline clutching at Etta possessively and narrowly missing.

'I don't think it's a competition, dear,' Daisy beamed as Etta nodded.

'What do friends do, usually?' Caroline asked suspiciously, clutching her spell-book to her stomach.

Etta rolled her eyes, 'They get together and discuss things like we are doing right now, they have tea, they borrow each others things, like the time you let me use your wand to test the invisible wall...or me lending you my dress...' Etta said and got Caroline nodding and visibly relaxing.

'I'm still not lending you my spell-book. Or my wand.' Caroline told Daisy.

Daisy took her wand out of her apron pocket and said, 'You can borrow mine, if you like. What invisible wall?'

Etta and Caroline filled her in. Etta also told the both of them that according to the mouse this neck of the woods had been much more populated once.

'It sounds like this patch of forest has been cleared for a reason...' Etta voiced her conclusion.

'By whom?' Caroline asked.

'The Fairy Queen?' Etta offered as the other two stared at her.

'Why would you even suggest such a thing?' Caroline asked.

'Judging how she did by you, she is not exactly the reliable or caring kind, is she? Also, she seems to feature a lot in this story we are in,' Etta said. 'She put you up with the Beast and she might have performed the mouse's marriage ceremony. Plus she has some deal going on with the May bugs.'

'That's all you've got?' Daisy asked. 'Why would a Fairy Queen with a lovely colony of her own keep fairies incarcerated against their will?' Daisy asked another obvious question. 'I doubt the three of us did something really bad when we were little. No. It seems this would be the doing of someone who didn't particularly like fairies or maybe was trying to get back at the Fairy Queen for some reason...'

'But I heard the queen confessing she tasked the bugs to goad fairies!' Etta said.

'I don't believe you,' Daisy said.

'Maybe the hag was the villain all along?' Caroline offered.

'I doubt it,' Etta said.

'The similarities in all of our fates started after our stay with her,' Caroline pointed out.

'The frog, the butterfly, the May bugs, the mouse for the

two of us,' Etta gestured at herself and Daisy, 'but not for you,' Etta told Caroline.

'Hang on. What about when the similarities ended?' Caroline asked.

Etta said, 'You two were pulled away from here when...'

'When I used the wand when I couldn't handle the cleaning,' Daisy said.

'Despite being told to use it only in emergencies?' Etta asked and Daisy nodded. 'You were then made a fairy godmother to Cinderella who...'

'Always cleans,' Etta and Daisy said in unison.

'Caroline, you were goaded over your looks,' Etta said, waiting for Caroline to connect the dots.

When she didn't, Etta finished, 'And then had to bestow a daily curse that transformed a good-looking boy into a hideous beast...again, about the looks, don't you think?'

Caroline shrugged.

'And I'm still here, my patience being tested to the limits with the stupid idea of having to marry a mole,' Etta said.

'You said tested. Maybe we are all being tested?' Caroline suggested.

'We were whisked away after we did something we shouldn't have done,' Daisy added. 'I used the wand to clean and you...died?'

'It was as if we were removed after we had failed some sort of test and we were then made to do penance for our failures.' Caroline mused.

Etta wondered what would happen if she refused to make her dowry and flat out refused to wed the mole.

'But you said there were about ten sheds. What happened to the rest?' Caroline asked another obvious question.

'Are you sure you never saw the evil hag cooking and eating any fairies in the house?' Daisy asked.

Etta shook her head, 'Nope. Besides, don't you think if she had such culinary preferences and got hungry, I would have been her prime temptation?' Etta said.

'Yohoo!' Cinderella waived at them through the portal, 'If you're done chatting, can you send my godmother back? We need to do stuff, the guests are almost upon us.'

'Well, I'd better get back there,' Daisy said hesitantly and rose.

Etta grabbed her hand, 'By the way, do you know where 'there' is?' she said nodding her head at the kitchen on the other side of the 'magic mirror'.

'It's a fairy-tale, that's all I know and that's enough for me!' Daisy laughed.

Etta held on, 'Yes, but do you know WHERE this particular fairy-tale is taking place?'

'Well, yes!' Daisy brightened, 'I believe it's the Magic Kingdom, although I have yet to see it since we mostly stay here, in this kitchen...or this house... We are yet to get to the castle, but once we do, then there we shall stay, although I'm pretty fuzzy on what happens AFTER the happily ever after when Ella weds her prince...' Daisy looked perplexed.

Etta sighed and let go of her.

Daisy obviously didn't know. Besides, the WHERE didn't matter, with the Excio spell and her repaired wand she could now always get to where Daisy was. Always.

'Once you get to the castle, you'll probably be promoted to nappy-changer,' Etta told Daisy and stuck out her tongue.

Cinderella 'oi-d' loudly and sat down into the dirt.

'Well, what did you think happens after marriage? A wedding night. And what happens then...' Etta teased as the girl buried her dirty face into her even dirtier hands.

'Don't even go there,' Daisy said primly, lifting up her skirts. 'Ella is not that kind of girl.'

'Oh, honey, after marriage it's her royal duty to be that kind of girl,' Etta said and patted Daisy on the head, 'How else is she going to produce an heir and a spare?'

Chapter 35. The Glitch

Daisy rolled her eyes. 'We shall meet again soon, yes? Say tomorrow?' She got nods. 'And how do I get in touch with you two? Will you open the magic mirror passage for me again?'

Etta scribbled the *Excio* spell down one more time with both names and pronunciation and handed it to Daisy. 'Here, just say that and that magic mirror will open again into here or into Caroline's abode.'

Daisy nodded and stepped across, back to Ella's kitchen.

Caroline was carefully enunciating from the slip of paper. Another portal opened up next to the gateway into Daisy's kitchen and Etta saw Caroline's living room. Caroline waved and off she went, with the spell-book under her arm, still wearing Etta's light-blue dress.

As the portal closed behind Caroline, Etta watched the one still open.

Ella's kitchen, grimy as it was, looked inviting and warm and cosy.

The open portal beckoned.

If travelling between places was so easy, Etta didn't see a point remaining with the mouse who had turned into yet another captor. Any other place, wherever it was, was better than here!

'Daisy, wait!' she said, 'Can I come with you, please?'

Before Daisy could say anything, the gateway into the kitchen closed with a loud pop, eliciting a pause in the snores next door.

Maybe there was a time-lag on the portal to allow safe passage and she had narrowly missed it.

No biggie, she could open another one.

'*Excio Daisy!*' Etta said and pointed at the space where the portal had been moments before.

The snores in the next room resumed, increasing in volume.

The air refused to budge.

Not again!

Etta looked at her blue wand.

She was pretty sure she had used her own wand for the unlocking and the Excio spell to summon Daisy.

'Very well, *Excio Caroline!*' Etta said.

No portal.

Right...

Time to test if the unlocking spell still worked, now that Caroline was gone.

'*Aperio!*' she told the cupboard door.

The door clicked and creaked open.

Etta walked to the front door.

'*Aperio!*' she said and heard a click.

'*Claudere!*' she ordered and heard another click.

She yanked on the door.

It was shut.

The wand COULD do new spells.

Just not the Excio spell.

Caroline had made her own portal appear and it had closed neatly after she had left.

Etta had opened the one to Daisy's and it had remained open for close to an hour and just as Etta had decided to use it, the portal had closed.

As if someone had closed it under her very nose.

Etta got the strange sense that she was allowed to use common, not magic doors to get out of here.

She shook her head to clear it.

She HAD to get out of here.

Now.

She walked over to the mouse's bedroom.

Her captor was still snoring loudly.

Etta tried to open the cupboard without making any noise.

First, she had to make a light-blue dress again to replace the one she had gifted Caroline.

There were only a few hours of the night left.

If she left now, she would only have a few hours head start and would probably freeze to death without a long dress.

If she left tomorrow night, she would get at least eight to ten hours of trek time ahead of the mouse.

She would make one dress and start another ball of yarn on the spindle, which would make it seem that Etta was still MAKING her dowry, which would mean she wasn't READY to marry the mole yet.

Postponing the damn ceremony was as important as planning her escape.

Tomorrow night, before she left, she'd leave the front door open and make some footprints outside to throw the mouse off.

After that she would venture into the tunnels and find a way to escape through the hole the mole had made.

Chapter 36. The Big Escape

The next night, walking through the tunnel in the pitch black, fingering the rough walls for support, Etta cursed the mouse for hiding the lantern away somewhere Etta couldn't find it. It could really have helped her to see where she was going.

She head chirping.

A bird?

The sound reverberated through the tunnel.

If the sound was this loud, she was close to the hole.

Very close.

Etta went around a corner and saw a faint light.

Almost there!

Etta pressed herself against the wall.

The tunnel seemed empty.

Etta crept closer.

And closer.

'Tweet-tweet!' Came from up top.

Etta threw the rope up at the hole and said, *'Applico!'*

When she was sure the rope was firmly secured - to what, she didn't know and didn't care - she climbed out of the hole.

'Finally!' Etta mumbled as she collapsed onto the frozen ground.

She was breathing fresh air under the vast sky and even though the moon wasn't at its brightest, it was still there!!

Etta grinned.

A giant shadow loomed over her.

'Tweet-tweet! Hello, little girl!' the swallow said.

'Oh, it's you!' Etta said and smiled widely. 'Why'd you come back?' she asked and squinted up at the bird. *Maybe swallows got lazy or lost their navigation skills off-season? Or when they were undead?*

'I never said good-bye,' the swallow said.

'Oh...' Etta nodded.

'Also, I realised that I never asked you if you wanted to

come away with me,' the bird chirped. 'You nursed me to life and went to and fro with the mouse and the mole, so I thought you lived here and were happy. I've seen weirder living arrangements than a fairy, a mouse and a mole.'

Etta laughed so hard she felt the tears start.

'Muahha-haa-hhaa...living arrangement...it was more like a hostage and an arranged marriage arrangement...' Etta hiccoughed.

'But you never said an unkind word about them behind their backs...the whole time you were tending me,' the bird said.

To an unconscious bird? What would have been the point? Etta thought.

She shivered in the icy wind and moved closer to the bird.

'So, you're not happy and you want to come away with me?' the bird asked.

'Yes, please!' Etta said.

'Hop on!' The swallow said, 'And I will take you far far away from here.'

Etta petted its plumage, 'So soft....'

When the bird laid out the same wing that had been broken Etta tried not to think she was climbing on top of a corpse.

A much better preserved corpse than Caroline, but a corpse nevertheless.

At least it didn't smell.

Yet.

When she was safely nestled in the furrows of the bird's neck it chirped, 'I'm taking you where my home is. Ready?'

'Yes!!' Etta shouted and they were off, gravitation pushing Etta further into the plumage and the roaring sound of air squeezing out any other sound.

So this is what it must feel like riding a fighter plane that the old woman had spoken of with admiration, Etta thought.

She dug in her heels and smiled, holding on as her rescuer took off and the trees and the woods and even the river faded into a carpet of white below them.

19.   'Hop on!' The swallow said.

Chapter 37. The Flowers

With the swallow flying higher and higher, above and beyond the wintry treetops, Etta took long deep breaths and welcomed the cold.

She was finally rid of the mole and the mouse and all their nonsense.

Etta was content huddling into her rescuer's neck.

The bird was now another discrepancy in the story she shared with Caroline and Daisy.

They flew for hours, it seemed.

She couldn't see much of what was below until she felt the first rays of the sun on her left cheek.

Etta recognised a familiar cleared field.

They were approaching the part of the woods separating her world from Caroline's.

The invisible wall...

Etta felt her heart start to beat faster.

She tugged at the bird who didn't seem to notice.

Annabel had said butterflies avoided it, but they could fly over the cursed place.

Etta hoped birds could, too.

Otherwise they were heading for a rather nasty crash.

Still, dying on impact when trying to escape was better than being married to a mole.

She tugged at the bird again.

No response.

Etta braced herself and squeezed her eyes shut, hoping the bird would make it.

Minutes later, she hazarded opening one eye.

The forest below was ... just a forest.

She didn't see Caroline's house.

'Are we in the Magic Kingdom?' Etta yelled.

She didn't get any reply this time either.

Soon, she didn't have time to think whether the swallow heard her yelps or not.

Below them, lay the familiar flower fields Etta had spotted the time Stephen flew them to the oak.

Etta felt snuggly warm.

Somehow, magically, they had abandoned winter for summer.

Etta was so happy, she hugged the swallow.

Perhaps it was the vibrant colours, but she had the strangest urge to tell the bird to land and set her free amidst the flowers.

Communication was a problem, though.

No matter how Etta tugged or yelled or even kicked at the swallow's neck, it was as if the bird didn't even sense she was there.

Had the bird simply forgotten her?

At noon, Etta felt tired from the merciless sun beating down on them.

She was pretty sure they were circling the colourful flower fields.

It was the same damn turquoise daffodils, peach forget-me-nots, pink daisies and orange callas.

Maybe circling was something swallows did?

Yes, but for the third time now?

Was the swallow searching for something specific or was it just lost?

She hoped she hadn't gotten out of one loop just to end up in another one.

At least they had left the oak behind.

Etta felt her stomach plummet as the swallow dived.

She held on for dear life.

The swallow dropped her off onto a pink daisy.

The bird circled back once to tweet its farewell. 'Good-bye, pretty girl! And good luck!'

Etta waved at it and thought, *Good luck with what?*

Chapter 38. The Proposal

'Oh, hello,' said a boy who was Etta's size and so delicate he looked almost translucent.

'Hi...' Etta said and couldn't help staring.

It was a boy!

With huge see-through wings!

The male fairy lowered his eyes.

She was inches away from a boy her own size!

A translucent, pasty, quiet and shy boy, by the looks of it, but a boy nevertheless.

Etta wondered if fairy boys were somehow different from Caroline or Daisy.

Of all the flowers the bird could pick, it had picked the one already occupied.

Now, why would it do that?

'You look like fun,' the boy said and winked.

Etta blinked back her surprise.

The translucent joker circled her like she was a prize cow.

'Hey, quit that! What are you, a vulture?' Etta asked.

'What's a vulture?' the boy asked, looking at her in wonder. 'And why did you have to use a bird to fly here, where are your wings?'

Etta shrugged, 'I don't have them. And the bird was kind enough...' *To finally put me down.*

'You don't have wings? Why? What happened to them?' the boy looked concerned.

'I was born like this...' she said.

'You were born crippled?' he asked, radiating concern.

'I wouldn't put it like that, exactly,' Etta said, getting cross. 'Why, were you able to fly straight from the cradle?' she asked him back.

'I guess so, I mean I don't remember...' the boy said, fluttering his wings.

'I see. Early Alzheimer's?' Etta shot back. When she saw that he didn't understand, she patted his arm, which seemed quite solid despite being pasty-white, and sighed, 'So young and already you have terrible lapses in memory...'

'No, I don't!' the boy huffed, 'Nobody remembers that far back in their childhood!'

I do Etta almost said and stopped herself.

'Besides, I could have you beheaded for this!' the boy puffed out his chest, 'Don't you know who you're talking to?'

'Should I? You never introduced yourself,' Etta shrugged.

Lovely manners, starting conversations with threats to behead before names were exchanged.

'Don't you know this flower is off limits to anyone but me?' the boy asked.

'No. I just flew in on a bird, in case you didn't notice. And why is it off limits? Are you incarcerated here or something?'

'Oh, I beg your pardon,' the boy smiled, 'You're a visitor. I'm Edwin, the crown prince of the flower colony of Terramara and this,' he gestured around him, 'is my private playground.'

A playpen? How old was the dude? He looked her age, but the way he was talking, she was starting to doubt appearances.

'Charmed,' Etta said, refusing to volunteer any more information.

In case she was on her way in five minutes, there was no point in overburdening the boy with information.

Even a boy who looked kinda good.

Because he acted awful!

'What do I call you? Pretty girl?'

If she didn't give her name now, it would be considered rude...and to royalty who could behead her if he wanted.

'Etta,' she said through gritted teeth.

If all fairy boys were like this, she'll have none of them!

'If next you tell me you'll have me beheaded because I didn't curtsy, I still won't curtsy. I'm not one of your loyal subjects and have no intention of bowing and scraping.'

'Oh no, we don't behead visitors,' Edwin laughed a tinkling laugh, which Etta to her horror found mesmerising.

'Yeah, just your own subjects,' Etta said and muttered under her breath, 'I wonder if they're loyal or just scared what with all the beheadings...'

'Would you like to be?' he asked in earnest.

'Be what?' Etta asked.

Beheaded?

'One of my loyal subjects,' Edwin said.

'No, thanks,' Etta replied, pretty sure it was up to her to make that decision.

'Well, then, would you care to dance instead? I love dancing! I've been practising all morning...' the boy's demeanour had completely changed from uppish to pleading.

'What to? There's no music,' Etta pointed out.

The prince waved his hand and crickets started chirping so loud Etta covered her ears.

'Tone it down! We don't want to scare our guest!' the prince ordered and the chirping became lower and slower.

'May I?' Edwin offered Etta his hand.

She hesitated for a second and then decided to take it.

Why not?

Beats cleaning the mouse's house after one of her episodes.

Halfway into the dance Etta looked up at the boy and said, 'You do a pretty decent waltz.' *She would know, having watched international ballroom competitions with the old woman on the television.*

'Thank you! I just learnt it today. Mama told me I should, just in case I might need to take a bride. At the wedding, it is customary to...' he tripped up and they both fell down with Etta on top of the boy.

Up close he didn't seem so pasty anymore.

He winked at her.

Or shy.

Etta felt her ears flushing.

'Waltz,' Etta said, 'At the weddings, it's customary to waltz.' She scrambled up, colouring to her roots, heart pounding from embarrassment.

'Sorry,' she said, 'I tripped.'

Etta fingered the wand in her apron to check it was still in one piece.

It was.

Edwin laughed, sitting up. 'For someone without wings, you're pretty...nimble,' he said assessing her from head to toe. 'And the wings situation...that could be rectified... Well, if you don't want to be one of my loyal subjects, would you consider marriage?' he asked, getting on his knees.

'Marriage to whom?' Etta asked on autopilot, not being able to help herself.

'Me,' Edwin said, grabbing her hand. In the same breath, he sprang up and lifted the listless Etta mid-eyeroll into another waltz as the crickets kept chirping.

***

When the boy finally stopped dancing and let go of her, Etta straightened her apron and prepared herself for a serious talk.

She cleared her throat.

'Look...Edwin, was it? ... I don't mean to be rude, but... where did you get an idea that I'm A. single, B. interested or C. good marriage material?' Etta asked, hoping he would see reason and recant his foolish proposal as a joke.

'You and I dance well together,' Edwin said and took a few dancing steps by himself.

'Great! As far as I know, it takes a little bit more than good dancing skills to make a good marriage,' Etta said.

'I like you,' Edwin said.

'That's very nice. I should think it's important that I also like you, don't you think?' Etta asked. 'Or love you, even.'

He stopped twirling, 'Well, don't you?' he asked wide-eyed and innocent. 'What's not to love?'

'It's too early to tell, I don't even know you,' Etta said.

'Oh,' he was deep in thought. 'Very well, I shall procure a few good character witnesses, so you can decide,' he said and waved at someone.

Etta felt a familiar whoosh sweep her hair across her face. *Butterflies?*

'Oh, my goodness, aren't you a cutie!' gushed a fairy with yellow wings, hovering above them.

'And pretty as a picture!' said another one, flapping her pink wings as she landed onto the flower.

'Hello?' Etta said and smiled.

'Good choice,' the fairy with the pink wings told the prince. *Hey, what was she, cattle?*

Before Etta could ask anything, the owner of the yellow wings turned to the prince, 'You know what would make her even more gorgeous?'

Oh no, here we go again.

20.   *'Marriage to whom?'*
'Me!'

Not just the May bugs, but fairies, too, were mean?

Some character witnesses.

The fairy snapped her fingers.

Two more fairies in considerably more drab attire approached carrying the most beautiful white wings Etta had ever seen.

'The wings are from a dragonfly. A dead one. You must realise. They were so beautiful we couldn't resist...' the fairy with the yellow wings said.

'I knew they'd come in handy!' said the one with the pink wings.

'These,' the fairy with yellow wings said, 'Are for you. Do you accept?' she asked.

Without question!

Etta nodded, starry-eyed. 'I do!' she breathed out.

Three things happened at once.

Etta reached out.

The wings shied away.

The servant fairies let go of the wings and left without uttering a word.

***

When she saw the wings plummet, Etta wanted to call the horrible fairies by all the nasty names she could think of.

Why would they dangle them in front of me and tell me this was my gift when they always meant to destroy them?

When the wings hovered inches from the ground and slowly wafted back to the flower, Etta exhaled, relieved.

The wings floated closer.

Tantalising.

Inviting.

Once more, Etta reached out her hand.

The wings shied away again.

A bit less this time.

If they were sentient, maybe they were like scared animals.

Etta kept holding her hand out.

The wings floated a little bit closer and brushed against her fingertips.

Score!

The wings floated upwards, dancing around Etta.

She laughed.

They kept circling her, inching closer and closer.

All Etta could see was the spinning cocoon around her.

It felt like a caress.

A rather possessive one, at that.

It felt like the wings were wrapping themselves around her.

For a moment Etta felt suction on her back, in between her shoulder blades.

An electric current seared through her.

So, that's how it felt...

Done absorbing Etta, her wings, HER wings, folded out and relaxed.

Etta adjusted her posture to the newfound weight.

'Wow! You look magnificent!' the prince said.

'Thank you,' Etta said.

'Marry me!' he said.

'Not with the marriage thing again!' Etta rolled her eyes. 'What happened to wooing? I mean you started with a gift and that's nice, but what about getting to know each other over flowers, chocolates, dancing, dining...that kind of thing...?' she mused, trying to remember the romantic comedies the old woman used to love so much.

Maybe if she was high maintenance, he would back off?

'Besides, although I do like what your 'character witnesses' just did!' Etta made quotations marks with her fingers, 'But that's more of a bribe than vouching for your character, you know,' she told Edwin and said 'Thank you!' to the fairies.

The prince laughed.

'She's a sharp one, she is,' the fairy with the pink wings said and sprang into the air. 'Bye, see you at the party!' she said as she whooshed away.

'Party? What party?' Etta asked the remaining fairy who looked pointedly at the prince.

'Flowers - you can have any one you want. To peruse as your new home. My gift to you,' the prince said spreading his arms wide. 'Any flower in my kingdom. Which one do you like?'

Wow. As far as grand gestures went...this boy didn't waste time...first the wings, now a house?

'Cho-cco-lattes - I don't know what those are, but we'll learn to make them for you. I'll order my kitchens immediately,' he waved and the other fairy flew off.

Presumably to the kitchens.

'Dancing and dining - would you do me the honour of accompanying me to our annual Spring Ball tonight, my dear?' Edwin bowed.

Etta thought for a second and then nodded.

Well, why not?

A party was better than cleaning the mouse's kitchen.

A party was better than being undead.

Edwin smiled and extended his hand. 'Shall we?'

She had an almost functioning wand AND a pair of magnificent wings.

If she didn't like the ball, she was free to fly wherever she wanted to.

And maybe look for Caroline and Daisy.

After she learnt HOW to fly.

The prince's hand was still outstretched.

Right there for the taking.

Did he expect her to fly right now?!?

Oh, hell's bells!

Etta sighed, gave Edwin her hand and let him lead her to her first flying lesson, her new house and her new life.

Chapter 39. The Ball

The morning after her arrival in Terramara, Etta was looking at a reflection of herself clad in something white and poufy.

The mirror etched in swirls and interwoven plaits barely contained the image of white taffeta of indescribable volume.

Ancient Celtic mirrors didn't lie.

Why would they?

Last night at the ball, the prince had proposed again.

At midnight.

In public.

On one knee.

With his mother looking on.

Apparently, fairies were a rather impulsive species.

That she could believe.

What she couldn't believe was that she had said 'yes'.

From then on, the annual Spring Ball had quickly turned into an engagement party.

And now, a mere day later, on the prince's 18th birthday, there was going to be a wedding.

Her wedding.

To the prince.

Of an entire kingdom.

Who was next in line for the throne.

Which meant she would be queen some day.

All she had to do was say 'Yes' to him again.

In public.

In an hour.

Etta shook her head to clear it and her tiara almost fell off.

Adjusting her headdress, Etta kept staring at the bride in the mirror.

Who was that girl?

Just yesterday morning, she had been a servant and prisoner of a forgetful mouse.

She still didn't know why she had said yes.

Was it from curiosity?

Was it from the compulsion to avoid embarrassment that came with saying 'no' to a very personal question in a very public place?

Was it because Edwin was actually a good guy and she liked him?

As in liked *him liked him?*

Etta fluttered her wings at the memory and shook her head again.

Last night, she had barely arrived at the banquet hall when the prince had pranced up to her.

'Well, hello, gorgeous!' he said and smiled.

'Hello!' Etta said, 'Am I supposed to bow or curtsy or something?' she asked, folding her wings to fit through the double doors.

'Well, I don't expect you out of all fairies to stand on ceremony, darling,' he took her by the hand, 'but Maman does.'

Maman? She was about to meet the queen?

He led her to the intensely decorated throne set up on a dais.

Quite a feat, if you considered they were having the ball in a giant tulip, Etta thought.

'Ah, our very special guest,' the queen said, looked elsewhere and extended her hand for kissing.

That voice!

What were the chances?

Etta felt her newfound sense of freedom dimming.

To hide her confusion, she coughed, shook the proffered hand, then curtsied, looking the queen straight in the eyes, 'Pleased to make your acquaintance, Your Majesty,' she said.

Finally.

The queen laughed a tinkling laugh, assessing Etta from head to toe from under her long dark lashes, 'Well, you do know how to address royalty, so I'm going to assume you shook my hand on purpose.' The queen smiled and said, 'For the future, I prefer Morgana.' To her son she said, inclining her head, 'I like her, she has...spunk. My job here is done,' Morgana sighed and rose, 'I'm going to go try some of that chocolate cake I see. You kids have fun!'

The boy swept Etta up into a waltz.

'So we have Maman's approval,' he said, spinning her round and round the floor.

'Approval for what?' Etta asked on autopilot. 'I didn't her approve of anything.'

'Our marriage, of course,' the prince responded.

Why was everyone hell bent on marriage?

Etta forced a smile and distanced herself slightly from the boy's embrace, 'Listen, buster...'

'Edwin,' he corrected her. 'That is if you agree to marry me, if not, it's Prince Edwin,' he smirked.

'Listen, Prince Edwin,' Etta continued.

'Ooh, sounds like you need a little more coaxing,' the boy said, steering her towards the desserts cart. 'Chocolate fudge? Or chocolate cake? Or sachertorte?' he asked.

'Wow! This morning you didn't know what chocolate was, now you have chocolate fudge and sachertorte?' Etta looked suitably impressed.

'It was the kitchens, but yes. I had them look up some recipes,' he said and smiled at her again, then leaned in and whispered, 'Not all from our Terramara, by the way.'

'Uh-uh. You call this SOME?' Etta gestured at the long row of a wide variety of chocolate cakes laid out for her enjoyment, apparently.

'Anything for my princess,' the boy said and attempted to take her by the hand.

'Listen, Prince Edwin, I am NOT your princess and I don't INTEND to be your princess unless you give me a good reason and there can be only one good reason to get married,' Etta said sternly, remembering the old woman's teachings.

'Of course. You're talking about love,' the boy said and grabbed her waist, returning them to the dance floor in a backward spin.

Etta had no choice but to follow, 'Yes. Love.' She said.

'Well, what makes you think I don't love you?' he asked.

Etta furrowed her brow.

This was the strangest conversation.

'You've never told me that you loved me. It's not like you've swept me off my feet and I'm all starry-eyed and goo-goo-crazy-for-you. For a start, love needs time to develop. On my part anyway,' the last bit she mumbled.

'Well, let it develop then,' the prince said. 'As for me, consider me swept off my feet, starry-eyed and goo-goo-crazy,' he smiled.

Etta smirked, 'Seriously? Are you saying you fell for me the minute you laid your eyes on me this morning?' she asked.

'Yes, my dear, that was it! I fell the minute YOU laid your eyes on ME,' he smirked.

'I don't believe you,' Etta said.

'Didn't I propose to you when we met?' Edwin asked, holding her right hand to his chest and looking into her eyes.

'You did,' Etta admitted. 'Proposals usually came AFTER both parties fall in love, don't you think?' she said, remembering all the romantic movies she had watched with the old woman.

'Have you had much experience with proposals?' Edwin asked and Etta shook her head.

'Me, neither!' the prince admitted. 'So, how would I know anything about who is supposed to do what and when?' he asked. 'Do you think I go proposing around to anybody and everybody, darling?' the prince asked.

'I don't know. Do you? Both ways means I should be in love with you as well. And I'm not,' Etta said. I haven't even had the chance to meet, much less to ask anybody about you.' Etta pointed out.

The dance ended. The prince looked thoughtful. He nodded, 'You are, of course, quite right,' he said and dragged her off to meet everyone.

Because, of course, everyone who was anyone was at the ball that night.

A sea of faces, names, bows and curtsies later, Etta had to hand it to the prince. Nobody had a bad word to say about him. And it wasn't like they were singing him accolades out of fear either. When Edwin had introduced her to the first couple of fairy aristocrats, he discreetly excused himself and let her be ushered on and entertained by his courtiers.

Giving her some space was also rather thoughtful.

Etta watched him across the room, joking with his mother.

Morgana.

A strange name from a strange tale the old woman used to read to her.

She couldn't bring herself to call the kind old woman a hag when thinking about her, gilded cage or not.

Edwin threw his head back and laughed that tinkling laugh of his at something his mother said.

Regardless of how she had tricked Caroline, she looked like a doting mother.

As far as mothers go, she was only the second one Etta had met. Fifth, if she counted the frog mama and the two butterflies.

Morgana and Edwin had both welcomed her to their kingdom and their annual Spring Ball.

Everybody she had met here had been very hospitable.

The kitchens had exceeded themselves with the chocolate cake selection.

For her.

Forget about the cakes, they had given her wings!

Etta looked at Edwin.

The boy was pleasant to look at. The way he lighted up every time he looked in her direction made Etta believe he did really care for her.

The old woman had sometimes talked about love at first sight.

Maybe that's what had happened to Edwin.

True love couldn't be planned, could it?

So, if he had fallen in love at first sight, maybe she could fall in love at second sight?

If not, a divorce would solve all problems of unwanted marriages, as she had seen many a time on the old woman's television.

Etta shook her head out of last night's reverie.

She hiked up her skirts and adjusted her wand at her thigh.

She had requested a garter just for this purpose.

Since she hadn't spotted any other fairy sporting a wand, she had thought it wise to conceal hers.

Etta straightened, fluffed her veil in the mirror and exhaled.

One tiny question and a three-letter answer later, here she was.

Maybe being married to a prince would not be such a bad thing?

With her newly found wings, she could now fly wherever she wanted to.

But why fly everywhere alone?

Chapter 40. The Book

The book fell through the petals of the tulip serving as the roof of Etta's new royal chamber. She barely caught the hefty volume.

'A Collection of Fairy-tales'.

Etta ran a finger along the binding of the spine.

Genuine leather.

It reminded her of some of the volumes in the old woman's house.

She had never seen this one, though.

The fairy clutched the book to her chest, closed her eyes and inhaled its scent.

Dusty and musky with a hint of a flowery perfume.

Etta hazarded opening it.

When two hours later dainty bells jingled in the distance, she was still reading, cosily tucked into her armchair, in her wedding dress with the veil draped over her shoulders for comfort.

The ringing of the bells didn't register at first.

When it did, Etta dropped the book and flew out of the window towards her new life only to find Edwin exiting the chapel with a pretty blond bride on his arm.

Etta paused mid-flight, her mouth a round neat 'O'.

After waiving the newlyweds off in their carriage made of daisy petals and drawn by two swallows the queen flew to Etta's side. 'I'm afraid you were late, dear,' Morgana said, 'And to your own wedding.' She shook her head and tsk-tsk-ed.

Etta looked puzzled, 'I don't understand. Edwin proposed. Yesterday. Twice. How could he have wed someone else just because I was a little late to the ceremony?'

'You call two hours 'a little late'?' Morgana raised an eyebrow.

'You call two hours enough time to fall in love? Or did the prince have himself a standby bride?' Etta spat.

'Careful, you are starting to sound spiteful, dear. And if you consider that it took him only one dance to propose to you then yes, two hours is plenty of time from meet to marry. A complete stranger, as it happens. An outsider, who just happened to drop in and charm his socks off. Quite literally it would seem,' Morgana's mouth drew into a fine line.

'But Edwin told me yesterday that he loved me,' Etta said.

'Did he now? Did he really?' Morgana asked.

Etta tried to remember.

Edwin had said he liked her and then joked about love.

'What's not to love?'

He had showered her with gifts and gone all-out with the wooing, sachertorte included after SHE had suggested that's what she wanted.

When at the ball, she had pointed out that he had never told her he loved her, what had he said?

'Consider me swept off my feet, starry-eyed and goo-goo-crazy.'

Word for word how SHE had described love looked.

To her.

Based on the movies she used to watch.

He had never actually told her how he felt.

She had ASSUMED it was love at first sight.

Out loud Etta said, 'But he proposed.'

And hoping that in time she would also fall in love, she had accepted.

'That just shows determination to marry, not necessarily determination to marry you, dear,' Morgana said.

'So, he would marry a random stranger who happens to cross his path?' Etta asked.

Morgana smiled, 'You were also a stranger when you crossed his path.'

'Maybe I can count myself lucky I didn't marry your philanderer of a son...' Etta said.

'Careful, dear,' Morgana touched Etta's puffy sleeve that was starting to unravel. 'It's understandable. He was on a deadline. It's his eighteenth birthday, after all,' she said and waived Etta off.

'What does coming of age have to do with marriage?' Etta asked.

Morgana paused, 'Quite right. Bred in captivity, you wouldn't know a first thing about fairies.'

Bred in captivity?

How did she…?

Meanwhile, Morgana continued, 'How would you know about fairy traditions? He is the crown prince. When a fairy crown prince comes of age he has to take a queen.'

'And if he hasn't found anyone to his liking during the, oh, eighteen years of his existence and the girl he picked kept him waiting for a little and he was on a deadline, suddenly anyone would do?!?' Etta's hands went to her hips, 'Opportunistic, forgetful, fickle…'

Morgana shrugged and said 'Fairies, dear. Just fairies. Get used to it.'

'I don't want to get used to it! If fairies are so fickle, I wish I wasn't a fairy!' Etta said and clapped a hand over her mouth.

I didn't mean it, honestly, she thought.

Maybe her wings wouldn't fall right off…

'Wish granted,' Morgana nodded and Etta blinked. 'Shame. Out of all of the girls you showed the most promise. Who knew that it would be the last stumbling block that would derail you…'

Out of all the girls?

Bred in captivity?

Stumbling blocks?

Etta suddenly realised why there had been ten sheds in the old woman's back yard.

Why breaking the rules meant elimination.

In 'The Princess and the Pea' the queen had wanted to make sure her son married a princess and she had placed a pea under the gazillion mattresses.

All she got was a spoilt brat who could feel that pea through all those mattresses.

What had this queen tested for?

Etta thought of Caroline and Daisy and the ten sheds.

Brides.

No, bride candidates.

'There were more bride candidates besides me.' Etta said rather than asked. 'How many?'

'Twelve. With you, there were twelve,' Morgana shrugged.

Twelve?!?

What had happened to the other nine girls?

'Twelve. And he still wed number thirteen,' Etta said. 'All your best laid plans gone to waste. I guess you can't plan true love, after all.'

'Remember what I said about spite?' Morgana asked. 'Any more of it and I'll have trouble placing you in a decent fairy-tale.'

'Placing me?' Etta echoed as the queen nodded.

'Well yes. I thought it would be...educational if each of the girls who...stumbled was placed in a fairy-tale where they would have an opportunity to get over their stumbling block,' Morgana studied Etta carefully. 'What else was I going to do with those who failed?'

'Murder them...?' Etta mumbled. 'Then resurrect them and watch them die a slow decomposing death...?'

'Oh, so you've met Caroline,' Morgana said.

A strand of the neverwed bride's hair turned purple. 'Oh, look, consequences,' the queen held the strand up for the girl's inspection.

Etta shrugged. 'Where'd you place them?'

Daisy was in the Magic Kingdom and Etta didn't have much time to find Caroline, so any tips were welcome.

'You are an inquisitive one, aren't you?' Morgana said. 'What you really should be enquiring about is where I will be placing you.'

Etta bowed, 'If it may please your Majesty...' she remembered how Stephen's grovelling had helped. 'Perhaps you could do me the courtesy of letting me know where you've sent all the others...so that I could maybe try to guess what you might have in store for me...?...Guessing is more fun than just being told, don't you agree?' Etta smiled.

'Very well. If you're stalling, it won't work. There is no stalling this. Anyway, I see no harm in telling you,' the queen said. 'The first girl..'

'Do you not know their names?' Etta said, smiling through gritted teeth, 'Or don't you remember?'

Do you even care?

'What did I say about watching it?' Morgana said, 'Now, look what you've done to your hair!' and Etta glanced in the mirror.

Purple streaks lined her otherwise jet-black hair.

Etta shrugged it off, 'It looks fine to me. What happened to the others?'

Morgana smiled. 'Tenacious. I like you. Very well. The first girl got bored when rowing on the plate the old woman had left out for her. She ended up as the Tooth Fairy.'

'Because...?'

'Karma. As boredom prevented her from being happy and living a full life, she got given the opportunity to be busy and no fairy is busier than the Tooth Fairy.'

Etta nodded.

'The second one was immobilised when she woke up on the water-lily that the toad had deposited her on. She ended up as a princess. Rapunzel.'

'Fear of open spaces and she gets an opportunity to battle claustrophobia. In a tower. For years.'

'Watch it!' The queen said and pointed at Etta's feet.

One of her dainty white silk shoes had turned into a black combat boot.

'The third one was unable to cry to elicit the help of the fishes. She ended up as the princess in the Goose girl who has to weep buckets. The fourth one could cry alright but was unskilful in taming the butterfly. She became the Fairy Tulip in the White Doe fairy-tale, looking out for the princess who had been turned into a doe.'

'You transported all of them into fairy-tales to pay penance just because they couldn't follow some silly script of yours?' Etta asked, noticing out of the corner of her eye that in the mirror, her white wedding dress had turned into something short and black.

'Would you rather have them be carried off by the toad and end up as a morsel of food once they refused to marry the toad's son?' Morgana asked and was met with silence. 'I didn't think so. Now where was I? The fifth believed the cockchafers when they said that she was ugly. To cure that I turned her into the Enchantress in the Beauty and the Beast.'

Etta nodded.

Caroline the undead.

Out loud she said, 'So she would understand beauty is just skin deep - well, once some poor girl fell in love with the Beast despite his looks.'

'You're sharp. If only the blondie my son married had half of your smarts....' The queen sighed.

'Can't have it all, can you?' Etta suggested.

'Do you want to hear it or not?' Morgana asked and Etta nodded.

'The sixth...ended up as the Fairy with Turquoise Hair who had to reassure Pinocchio on his journey as penance for being unable to cope with living in the woods by herself. The seventh was exceptionally bad at housekeeping, so I placed her as fairy godmother to Cinderella...'

Daisy.

Etta nodded.

Wait.

In between Caroline and Daisy there had been another fairy?

Where did that one go?

The queen lifted an eyebrow. When Etta didn't volunteer any information, she continued, 'Anyway... The eighth was bad at telling stories, she is now Scheherazade. The ninth failed to be kind to the swallow that fell into the mole's tunnel, she became fairy godmother to Princess Donkey Skin. The tenth...is now one of the fairies in Sleeping Beauty.'

'Because she refused to learn how to spin cloth...' Etta said.

'The eleventh was afraid to fly and is now whizzing after Peter Pan...' Morgana kept listing.

Etta remembered the graveyard of water-lilies.

There had been so many.

She had never counted them.

A realisation hit her.

'You had all of your...experiments for the lack of a better word - in parallel?!?' Etta asked.

How could she have missed all those fairies working at Missus Mouse's?!?

Sure, the trek to Caroline's had taken a few days and then the same time back, but in those few days Morgana had managed to get rid of five more fairies?!?

The queen shrugged, 'I've had to wait fifteen years and more to get all my ducks lined up, of course I did everything in parallel. Otherwise, if I had tested one girl per year, my boy would have had to wait thirteen years to marry and no man is that patient,' she said. 'Especially not fairy men. And I'd rather NOT deal with his illegitimate offspring or him getting married to godess-knows-who....'

Except now he was anyway, Etta thought and smiled.

'...Not to mention that would have meant finding and inducting six new mice and two new moles and probably a few more swallows...' the queen mumbled.

The swallow had also been in on it, Etta thought with sadness.

Was anyone, anything in this story real?

'So, the mouse, the mole and the swallow were all in on it?' Etta asked just for confirmation.

Morgana shrugged, 'Just like the frog, the butterfly and the May bugs.' She gave Etta a once-over. 'You pieced all of that together by yourself? How?'

Etta shrugged, 'Must be my vivid imagination.'

Or the fairy-tales the old woman used to read to her at bedtime.

'No wonder the book was the thing that failed you.' Morgana said. 'Like mother, like daughter.'

'You knew my mother?' Etta blinked back her surprise.

Could Morgana be the witch the old woman went to for help?

'Of course I did. I knew all of the mothers. You didn't think I'd let my son marry riffraff, did you? Otherwise, how, would I have known where to send the May bugs?' Morgana huffed and turned away.

'You mean my real mother? And you SENT the bugs? To orphan fairy girls, to orphan ME, on purpose?!?' Etta asked as more of her black locks turned purple.

Morgana didn't even flinch.

Etta remembered the queen's conversation over Caroline's dead body.

'Goading every fairy they meet...'

Morgana raised an eyebrow, 'How...'

'How could you?'

'It was May. The bugs were going to goad someone to death anyway. They always do. Every year. I just...optimised.'

'You optimised?!?' Etta stomped and instead of a click heard a thunk. Both of her dainty slippers had turned into combat boots.

'In my defence, you were not a sanctioned harvest. Which is why I was rather displeased to see you at the ball,' Morgana pouted. She cast Etta a contemptuous look, 'Too bad you have your dad's looks. Maybe that's why Edwin chose the pretty blond angel for a wife,' Morgana smiled tartly.

Etta blinked.

Of course, she had known her father, too.

'You only sent the May bugs to maraud the prettiest of households...' Etta said.

'Yours was off limits,' Morgana shrugged.

'But they took me anyway,' Etta said and Morgana shrugged.

'In a way, I'm glad you and Edwin didn't marry. You either wouldn't have had any children or they would have been defective, if born at all. I spared you a whole lot of heartache, believe me!' Morgana assured.

'Edwin and I...we are related?' Etta asked and Morgana nodded.

'Cousins,' Morgana said.

'The book...YOU dropped the book. You were trying to stop Edwin from marrying me.' Etta said.

Morgana nodded. 'My bedchamber is directly above yours and the walls...are petal-thin,' the queen said looking out of the window. 'So, making a book drop as if through the air... was the easiest thing.'

Etta nodded.

Her whole life had been orchestrated for somebody else's pleasure.

'So, why did you let him pick me, if you then made him ditch me?' Etta asked.

'I didn't know you were the last one left,' Morgana said.

'Are you saying you didn't have a choice?!? You HAD a choice! Eleven other choices besides me. You could have picked one of the other girls without your stupid tests! Instead you ruined lives!'

Twelve girls, parents, too.

'Thirty-six lives, to be precise. With twenty-four fatalities. Twenty-five, if you count Caroline. And all for nothing. You still ended up with a random stranger for a daughter-in-law.'

Etta closed her eyes and shook her head.

'Oh don't be sad. I did what's best for you, even at the expense of intellectual prowess of my own son's progeny,' Morgana said.

Etta put up a hand, 'Don't. Just. Don't.'

Silence fell.

'What was my mother like?' Etta finally asked, swallowing her disappointment.

Morgana shrugged, 'Lorelei was...something else,' she said, shaking her head. 'Smart. Like you. With a big heart and a lot of patience.'

'Why did you ask the bugs to goad her, if she was so special to you?' Etta asked.

Morgana inhaled sharply and straightened. 'Lorelei was my sister-in-law. I cared for her. Confided in her. I even helped babysit you when you were just a tiny little thing. I never realised she was insecure about her looks. She always looked so happy...' Morgana said and added, 'The bugs shouldn't have goaded her!'

'But they did. Because you wanted some twisted bride experiment so your son would have a perfect girl as a present for his eighteenth birthday, a meek future spouse bred in captivity....'

'No! I wanted someone resourceful, a fighter, someone who would find her way out of the enchanted wood, someone to help Edwin rule!' Morgana cast a glance at Etta. Don't you get any ideas about claiming the throne! Edwin is and always has been the first in line, then his issue and only if he has none or none survive, only then it's your turn. Which will never happen, you hear!'

'If it will never happen, why did you tell me about it?' Etta asked and leaned against the wall.

Morgana smiled, 'Blood relatives make excellent allies. I told you in case Edwin needs your help someday.'

'After all of this - him ditching me, you killing my parents, harvesting innocent young fairies and making them jump through hoops so your son would have a pre-selected AND tested bride to wed - you still think I would help him?!? Are you insane?' Etta asked.

'In time, you might feel differently about the family you have left,' Morgana said.

'You are NOT my family!' Etta said defiantly, blinking back tears. 'If you cared for my mother so much, why didn't you adopt me?'

'And have Edwin grow up and definitely fall in love with a blood relative with no possibility of good progeny? I don't think so,' Morgana said. 'Oh, don't be cross. Look, your lovely eyes have gone different colours now,' Morgana admonished.

Etta stared in the mirror.

One of her eyes was still green.

The other had turned purple.

The mirror brought back the memory of Caroline's and Daisy's portals...magic mirrors closing in her face.

'Did you also deliberately sever the connection to Daisy just when I was about to walk through?' Etta turned back to Morgana, narrowing her eyes.

Morgana shrugged. 'Daisy, wait! Can I come with you, please?' she mimicked Etta's voice perfectly. 'It is very helpful that you are rather vocal, dear,' she smiled.

'You eavesdropped?' Etta asked.

'Not really. Not all of it. Blah blah blah we could be sisters. I just had to make sure you followed the proper route. Who do you think sent the swallow to get you?' Morgana asked.

Etta made a mental note to keep things even more to herself than she had before.

She didn't even have to ask if Morgana was the one who had enchanted her wand NOT to perform the *Excio* spell. 'You made me follow a designed route so I would meet Edwin,' Etta said crossly. 'This was all for Edwin. This whole experiment of yours! So your progeny would stay in power!'

Morgana nodded, 'Now you're getting it.'

Etta balled her hands into fists.

'Why so grim? What's the problem, dear? I thought you liked your newly found freedom and wings?' Morgana asked. She sized the former bride up. 'And I think I know exactly where you'll find yourself at home.'

'Who do you want me to godmother, auntie? Etta said acidly. 'After reading these fairy-tales of yours, I don't particularly fancy being a helpless princess,' Etta gestured at the book.

'You are not suitable to be either a godmother or spouse to a ruling monarch.'

'Why is that?'

'You have transcended species it seems. All those scathing remarks...' the queen tsk-tsked. 'Look at yourself.'

In her mirror, an angry-looking fairy clad in black was staring back at Etta.

'What am I now?' The former bride asked defiantly.

'A pixie, dear. You're a pixie. They are VERY sharp-tongued, turn green with envy and are...rather unpredictable in their affections and actions,' the queen smiled.

'Better a pixie than a heartless fairy,' Etta said grimly.

'Oh, honey, I'm no fairy at all,' said the ex-Harpy and flashed her fangs, ready to step out through the large French windows of Etta's tulip.

If fairies were not only born, but could also be...made... for the lack of a better word...

Etta struggled between curiosity and loathing for the freak who had farmed twelve girls in captivity, then tried and tested them for the OPPORTUNITY of marriage to her only son.

Optimists, please go to Epilogue 1.

Pessimists, please go to Epilogue 2.

21. *'What am I now?'*

Epilogue I - Happily Ever After

Curiosity won.

'What were you before? A vampire? A harpy?' Etta asked.

Morgana stepped away from the window and tilted her head, 'Now where would an innocent little fairy like you have heard about harpies?'

'The old woman,' Etta said.

'What about her?' Morgana narrowed her eyes.

'She read me Greek myths and fairy-tales as bedtime stories when I was a kid,' Etta said.

'And vampires?' Morgana asked.

'We used to watch vampire movies on All Hallow's Eve,' Etta said, wondering where this was going.

'You know about Halloween...' Morgana said, nodding thoughtfully.

'Doesn't everyone?' Etta asked.

'No, honey, not everyone,' Morgana said, sitting down.

Morgana tilted her head, 'Out of all the fairies, you alone got to watch movies and hear the bedtime stories and discuss interesting things, didn't you?'

Etta looked at her grimly, 'I am aware the others did not discuss books and movies and didn't play adventure games nor learn about physics or genetics or the other disciplines. I have two questions. Did she have to treat the others badly and how would the knowledge of quantum physics help me be a princess?' Etta wondered out loud.

Morgana narrowed her eyes at her, 'How very interesting. She went completely off script... Now why would she do that?'

If the old woman did something she wasn't supposed to, perhaps not everything she had told Etta had been a lie. As for why...

'She had to look after twelve fairies for fifteen years, try loneliness on for size,' Etta muttered to herself. Out loud she said, 'I can only assume you told her I was royalty.'

Morgana shook her head. 'I did no such thing. I did make sure she treated you better than the others by telling her that you are the one she gets to keep.'

Morgana HAD been the witch the old woman had asked for a child...

When Etta's eyes goggled, Morgana shrugged, 'Oh, come now. As if I was ever going to keep that promise. As soon as the prince was wed to some other suitable candidate, I was going to come and get you and reinstate you to the royal household of Terramara.'

'I don't believe you,' Etta said.

The old woman had treated her better because...she had thought Etta would stay.

She had treated her like her own child.

'Believe me or not, that WAS the plan,' the queen said.

'But it isn't any longer?' Etta asked and got a head shake in return.

'You know too much. I wouldn't want you to...cause unrest at court. Besides, I wouldn't want to tarnish Lorelei's memory by producing a pixie as her offspring.' Morgana crinkled her nose.

'More like tarnish your bloodline. Who would want to procreate with Edwin's offspring if he has a pixie for a cousin?' Etta spat.

Morgana laughed, 'Now I almost wish you had married my son after all instead of that airhead!'

Etta rolled her eyes.

'Marriage, marriage, marriage. The old woman had been right, most females, no matter what species - human, toad, bug, mouse, butterfly, fairy - are obviously obsessed with it.' Etta said.

Morgana laughed again, 'I know where you will fit right in! They could definitely benefit from your keen observation skills and wouldn't mind your sass,' Morgana said.

'They?' Etta echoed.

'The angels.'

'No thanks, I wouldn't want to be stuck in another fairy-tale, auntie,' Etta said.

'Oh, this wouldn't be a fairy-tale, dear. This would be a job. Helping people, beings in various dimensions, opportunity to travel, using your wand, lording it over winged beings much much larger than you...'

'If you think I enjoy lording it over others, you don't know me at all,' Etta scoffed.

Morgana laughed, 'You have royal blood, so trust me, you will. Watchers...wielding that kind of power...in time...it corrupts.'

Maybe you, but definitely not me Etta thought, noticing she was seriously considering the insane fairy's insane proposition.

The Fairy Queen may be a tad unhinged, but at least she tried, in her own twisted way, to do right by the girls she had experimented on. She had placed them in fairy-tales where they had a purpose.

'Fine! But only if you tell me where to find Caroline and Daisy.'

'See! Assertiveness. It comes natural to you, doesn't it?' Morgana smiled. 'Wait here, I'll come back for you,' Morgana threw across her shoulder as she flew away.

What harm could it do, having a gander?

If she liked it, she would be indebted to the Fairy Queen, who would, doubtlessly, extract a pound of flesh in aid of her son.

But if she didn't like it, with her newfound wings she could always escape.

***

The Agency of Guardian Angels enchanted Etta as soon as she stepped foot in it. Winged beings, of all shapes and sizes darted around.

And the wings...feathered and of all the colours of the rainbow!

Hers looked puny in comparison, although they were two times her size.

'Here is where I'll leave you. Go there,' Morgana pointed up the white marble staircase, 'and the rest is up to you,' she said, stealing sideways glances. The queen's eyes goggled and when Etta turned to look, Morgana evaporated before Etta could ask anything.

Not on their good books, huh, auntie?

No matter, at least she had got her here.

Unless this was another one of her underhanded tricks.

Etta zoomed up the staircase.

The revolving door flashing black and white was spinning so fast, it was a wonder she wasn't cut in half when she darted through it, finding an opportune moment.

Two pairs of eyes, one set brown and the other baby blue were staring at her.

'Who the hell are you?' asked the owner of the brown eyes. *Strangely, she reminded Etta of the old woman. Except for the sari, she could have been her twin sister.*

Language and all.

A frown formed above the baby-blues. 'You are not dead. Nor were you invited. So, how did you manage to get to the Agency of Guardian Angels and come through these doors?' asked the man, who could easily have passed for a Greek god, if it wasn't for the rune-encrusted sword hilt sticking out from between his shoulder blades.

Correction, from between his folded wings.

'You're an angel,' Etta said, trying not to sound too awed.

'Yes, a guardian, while you are not,' the angel said and stole a glance at the lady who appeared to be his superior.

'I didn't hire her,' the lady shrugged.

'Well, why don't you? Hire me,' Etta said, 'I heard the Watchers have a vacancy.[3]'

***

Etta found Daisy as expected - bored.

'Aren't you tired of sorting out her messes?' Etta asked Daisy by way of a greeting, pointing towards Cinderella nodding off in the corner.

Daisy waved a wand to get the broom sweeping and ran to hug her, stopping mid-stride.

'Seeing you are both still in this kitchen and the ball should have been last night, I take it that it didn't go too well and marriage is not on the books just yet?' Etta asked.

'Wow, you look different,' Daisy said, taking in Etta's Goth chic getup, combat boots and all. 'And, no, the ball is tonight, we just spoke yesterday, don't you remember?'

Etta raised an eyebrow. *Really?* She hunhed at the realisation that time flowed differently where Daisy was.

'So, what happened to you in the space of the one day I didn't see you?' Daisy asked.

'Apparently this,' Etta gestured at her outfit, 'is what my spiteful tongue can do - transform me from fairy into a different species,' Etta nodded.

'You're a different species now?' Daisy asked and sat down.

Etta nodded, 'Pixie. Reportedly spiteful, very sharp-tongued, turn green with envy and unpredictable in their affections and actions.'

Daisy giggled, 'Well, no wonder then.'

Etta smirked, 'I have to agree on all counts but for turning green with envy. Never gonna happen. Although, I almost did when I saw all those fairies coming at me, every single one of them with wings and me, still wingless, standing next to royalty who proposed five minutes after he met me..'

As Etta recounted her adventures, Daisy's eyes goggled. For the time being, Etta decided to leave out most of her final conversation with the queen, especially the part about her bride experiment.

'And now, you're a Watcher?' Daisy asked, 'What exactly do you do?'

'What it says on the tin - I watch over all sorts of beings from 63 known and a few unknown dimensions, although there are only 16 priority screens, which is a little bit on the skimpy side, if you ask me...' Etta said. 'And I can freeze time, if need be, when I send an angel to help...'

Daisy's eyes filled with longing, 'Oh, I do hope you haven't come to gloat. I'm so bored I could scream! You know, I used to want to use the wand to help me do the 'menial tasks' as you would say. Now I have a new wand and all I get to use it for is menial tasks,' Daisy sighed. 'There has to be more to life than this!' she gestured around the kitchen.

Etta nodded, 'About that. Are you almost done here, helping Ella get her happily ever after?' she asked.

Daisy took a good look around and nodded, 'The ball is tonight. After that, Ella is as good as married anyway and won't need any more of my help. And it's not like she's going to be cleaning stoves where she is going...'

'What if there were more happily ever afters that you could help happen, would you be interested?' the pixie idly wondered.

'You mean helping more than just one princess?' Daisy asked, petting a dove that was separating lentils from ash.

'Helping more than one being - princess, dragon, pixie, pirate, anyone that needs helping...' Etta mused.

'That would be nice. Do you know anyone who is looking for such help?' Daisy gave a sad little laugh.

Etta nodded quickly, 'The Agency of Guardian Angels is. We need another Watcher. Interested?' she asked.

Daisy's eyes filled with tears and she almost suffocated Etta in her hug, 'Yes, yes, yes! I'd love to be more useful,' she said.

'Yes, let's make sure you are not promoted to a nappy-changer. Let's leave! With you gone, you will have performed your task and will become part of the lore here.' Etta suggested.

'Part of the lore,' Daisy sniffled, 'I like that. And I can keep being a godmother. From afar.'

'I'm part of no lore. All I have is one failed attempt to marry a fairy prince under my belt.' Etta mused.

One of twelve inconsequential orphan brides the Fairy Queen had raised as potential mates for her precious only son.

'But you should be,' Daisy nodded.

'Yes, yes, I should. Because lore and Etta go well together,' Etta smirked and nodded.

'You know, lore and Etta make a lovely name together. Loretta!' Daisy smiled.

'Loretta...' Etta said. 'I could reinvent myself as a Loretta at the Agency and create my own lore,' she suggested and Daisy nodded vigorously.

'That's an excellent idea, Loretta! I like it! I like it very much!' Daisy beamed.

'Tonight is your big night. I'll come back for you in the morning,' Etta said, echoing the promises the queen had made to Caroline.

Now that she had Daisy by her side, Etta felt better. Together, they could find Caroline and maybe the three of them could all stick together, discover the world with eyes wide open. For once, without the deceptive lure of a prince.

Epilogue II - Happily Never After

Loathing won.

'You might want to retract those before you show your face in public or you might scare your subjects half to death,' Etta made a face.

Morgana retracted her fangs. 'Thank you! Now I know where you will fit right in! They could definitely benefit from your keen observation skills and wouldn't mind your sass,' Morgana said.

'They?' Etta echoed.

'The angels.'

'No thanks, I already told you that I wouldn't want to be stuck in another fairy-tale, auntie,' Etta said.

'Oh, this wouldn't be a fairy-tale, honey. This would be a job. Helping people, beings in various dimensions, opportunity to travel, using your wand, lording it over winged beings much larger than yourself.'

'If you think I enjoy lording it over others, you don't know me at all,' Etta scoffed.

Morgana laughed, 'You have royal blood, so trust me, you will. Watchers...wielding that kind of power...over time...it corrupts.'

One less reason to stick around and listen to you.

'Wait here, I'll send a swallow for you,' Morgana threw across her shoulder as she flew away.

As if.

The unhinged fairy queen had tried designing the first fifteen years of Ella's life. She wasn't going to let her design the next fifteen. Or the rest of her life, for that matter.

Etta would bet her wand that the swallow had also been paying some sort of debt that finished with it depositing Etta on Edwin's flower.

Now that the swallow had paid its dues, maybe it wouldn't mind flying them away from here if she asked nicely?

It was time to go find Daisy and see if she had managed to marry Ella off and to see if Caroline was still in one piece.

***

A tiny thumbelina with prominent pixie ears peeked into Etta's hut.

So this is how the Weird One lived.

Her house was a mess.

Everything was too...neat.

Even the books were organised and hanging on some wooden contraption on the wall.

Books! The Weird One had books! How medieval.

Everyone knew no good ever came from reading books.

Pixie life was supposed to be all about frolicking, mischief and fun.

Apparently, not for the Weird One.

She was looking for *work*!

Fui!

Clearing her throat, the thumbelina braced herself for the famous wrath of pixies when interrupted (*pixus interruptus*), 'Ahem...'scuze me...'

Etta looked up and eyed the kid above her book.

Shocked over NOT being yelled at, the kid almost forgot why she was there.

'Is there anything in particular I can help you with, child?'

The young pixie snorted at the 'child', instantly regaining the famous pixie arrogance (*pixus arrogancia*) 'As if. A *fairy* is here. We can only assume she's looking for *you*,' the kid spat with scorn.

'Really? Why? No fairy ever wondered here before I arrived?'

'Whatever.' Etta wasn't sure whether it was an obscene gesture or a simple pointer of a direction that the kid flipped when off she went, singing the last of her message as she pranced away, 'Outside.'

Sighing, Etta put the book away.

Bye-bye learning how to cook with poison.

Bye-bye books on practical jokes.

She glanced out of her window and spotted a familiar blond figure darting amongst the flowers, looking into windows.

Uh-oh.

She'd better go and put a stop to it, otherwise there will be hell to pay.

She didn't need years of reproachful and embellished accusations about how 'her horde of fairies' once came to disrupt their carefully planned leisure-time.

Everyone was home, having lunch pollen, and there was no one in sight, but pixies liked to embellish, so the tale would be spun until it would become completely miraculous to the point of improbable. Heavens forbid someone was in labour anywhere and the kid would not be born translucent blue. Etta would never hear the end of it.

Plus she didn't want the outcast kid thus born to be thrust upon her to raise.

That would put a considerable kink into her job search.

And job attendance, when she found one.

Etta fluttered her purple wings in annoyance (*pixus disgruntus*) and flew outside to roll out the welcome carpet.

As the fairy approached, Etta smiled.

It was only a matter of time until they found her.

'Hey! I'm right here!' Etta said and waved.

'Oh, hello! I'm looking for someone,' the fairy said.

'Yes, I know. Me!' Etta nodded.

The fairy looked at her and made a face, 'No. I'm quite sure the girl I'm looking for looks nothing like you, except...except my spell keeps pointing me at this pixie colony for some strange reason and so far you're the only one who has deigned to speak to me...'

'Daisy. Trust me. You're looking for me,' Etta said and the fairy goggled.

'Etta? Is that you? But how?!?' Daisy looked aghast.

'Apparently this,' Etta gestured at her Goth-clad outfit, 'is what my spiteful tongue can do - transform me from fairy into a different species.'

'A different species?' Daisy asked and sat down in one of the rocking chairs on Etta's porch.

Etta nodded, 'Pixie. Reportedly spiteful, very sharp-tongued, turn green with envy and unpredictable in their affections and actions.'

'No wonder, I thought the *Excio* spell wasn't working,' Daisy shook her head.

'That one still doesn't work for my wand,' Etta said. 'Payback from the Fairy Queen for missing an opportunity she offered.'

'What did she offer?' Daisy asked.

'A job. Something called the Watchers at some strange agency of do-gooder angels saving beings across different realms. I didn't want to be indebted to her and ran away.'

'And?' Daisy asked.

'And - of course she found me. And gave me an earful about how I had wasted her time and her favours. Apparently, she exhausted a favour of getting to the agency, a one-time offer, and now, even if I wanted to go there, I can't. Nobody knows how to get there.'

'I'm sure you were wise to reject her offer. Look what happened to Caroline,' Daisy said.

'How...how *is* she?' Etta asked.

'Still dead. That's why I came to find you,' Daisy said. 'She has disintegrated into bits and pieces, but she's not dying. You don't know how creepy it is when her mouth falls off and she still keeps talking...' Daisy shuddered. 'I can't keep putting her back together again. She begged me to kill her, but I don't know how.'

'And I would?' Etta was taken aback.

'Well, did you hear the spell the Fairy Queen used to bring Caroline back from the dead?'

Etta nodded.

'Maybe there is a way to reverse it… or enhance it… or something! There has to be a WAY!' Daisy wailed.

Etta patted her arm, 'Easy, there. Don't panic! We'll think of something.'

Etta thought about it.

'Fire seemed to work for the leaves and butterfly remnants…'

'Yes, but technically, she's still alive!' Daisy looked worried. 'We can't burn her alive!'

'Maybe if we use the reverse spell on assembling lint to disassemble Caroline into dust and scatter her somewhere nice, maybe that would work?' Etta offered.

Daisy nodded enthusiastically. 'I knew it was a good idea to go find you!'

'As in - if Caroline wasn't in trouble you wouldn't have come looking for me?' Etta asked, one of her eyebrows climbing up her forehead.

'No, I would have. It's just Caroline needed me more urgently…' Daisy had the good sense to colour to her roots. 'I mean, we didn't know what had happened to you and figured you were transported into another fairy-tale, just like we were.'

Etta laughed, throwing back her head. 'That's…that's…I guess that's true.' She grew serious.

'What happened?' Daisy asked.

As Etta recounted her adventures, Daisy ooh-ed and aah-ed. For the time being, Etta decided to leave out most of her final conversation with the Fairy Queen, especially the part about her bride experiment.

'That's a lot of adventures,' Daisy said.

'Yes. To last me a lifetime,' Etta retorted.

'Don't say that. Do you even know how long fairies and pixies live?' Daisy asked and Etta shook her head.

'Well, we'd better find out then! Daisy said.

Etta nodded, 'But enough about me, what about you? Besides looking out for Caroline, what are you up to? Did you marry Ella off already?' Etta asked.

'Why, yes! It all went swimmingly. I'm quite content. With everything.' the fairy said and raised her chin.

'They didn't promote you to chief nappy-changer at the palace, did they?'

Daisy looked suitably horrified. 'No! I bowed out of that story as soon as Ella was married, but then there was another girl that needed help and another and that's how I ended up as...'

'Let me guess... A professional godmother?' Etta smirked.

'Don't laugh, it's not nice,' Daisy huffed.

Etta pointed at herself, 'Pixie. I'm not nice by definition.'

Daisy rolled her eyes.

'Ok, so you're a Fairy Godmother, rushing around, helping damsels in distress,' Etta said and added, 'I'm distantly related to the scary Fairy Queen who resurrected Caroline.'

'The Fairy Queen of which flower colony?' Daisy enquired.

'Terramara,' Etta said and heard a sharp intake of breath.

'That's one of the fiercest fairy colonies,' Daisy whispered. 'There are loads of stories. These fairies are reported to be scheming, cunning, best warriors...'

Etta thought back to the two fairies who gifted her the wings and had trouble believing.

But perhaps everyone believed because of what Morgana was like.

'...Well all, except for their prince.' They are said to be almost as nasty as...' Daisy stared at Etta and clapped a hand over her mouth.

'Pixies,' Etta finished for her. 'Daisy, you're allowed to tell the truth.'

Daisy still looked uncomfortable.

'Believe me, I know exactly how mean and nasty pixies can be. Do you think they welcomed me here with open arms?

Almost stoned me to death and the screeching...brrr...' Etta said.

'But how can you be a pixie? If you are a distant relative of the queen, you're fairy royalty,' Daisy pointed out.

Etta shrugged and gestured at her attire, 'I don't know how this happened. You see these wings,' she pointed behind her back, 'They used to be white and they welded themselves to me somehow. Just like I transcended species somehow, without anybody casting a spell, without using my wand. Just...getting angry at what the queen was telling me.'

When Daisy's mouth fell open, Etta nodded.

'That's how not nice I am. I'm still an orphan, though, same as you. Same as Caroline.'

Except I know my mother's name.

'Apparently, I am descended from someone called Lorelei,' Etta said.

Daisy closed her mouth. 'You are nice! You are! Caroline and I like you and it doesn't matter what anyone else thinks!' She patted Etta's arm. 'And, you know, Lorelei and Etta make a lovely name together - Loretta!' Daisy said.

'Great! Maybe I can put that on my job application. Maybe then they'll hire a pixie and maybe then Morgana wouldn't know to thwart my efforts at nice jobs,' Etta muttered.

Daisy assessed Etta from head to toe and then pronounced, 'I think there is magic in you.'

Etta blinked.

'That's why the wings accepted you and you transformed and maybe that's also why the queen doesn't want you to do anything meaningful. Because you would be good at it.'

'Anything meaningful that *I* chose. She wanted me to do plenty meaningful when that would have meant that I would be indebted to her,' Etta corrected.

Daisy took Etta's hand, 'I believe there is magic in you and you will do great deeds. That's why I have faith you and I can liberate Caroline from her...'

Disintegration?

'*...Fate.*' Daisy said, looking bright-eyed and bushy-tailed. 'You wanted a job, right? Well, start by doing an old friend a favour and help her die!'

'So I could put that on my resume?' Etta muttered horrible pixie curses (*pixus cursus horrificus*).

'Why not?' Daisy asked and Etta looked at her like she was deranged.

'Warrior princesses do heroic things.'

Euthanasia was so not heroic, Etta thought.

'And you ARE a princess. So go do great deeds! Start with Caroline,' Daisy suggested.

Etta narrowed her eyes at the fairy, 'I know why you're good at the godmothering thing. You give a hell of a pep-talk.'

Daisy beamed and Etta thought, *Why the hell not.*

She had been itching to do something for a while now. Scattering Caroline to the winds was as good a place to start as any.

Sky's note

Thank you for reading this book!

I hope you liked it.

Like Etta, I am a huge fan of fairy-tales – traditional, retold, sweet and slightly creepy. The idea for this book came when re-reading Andersen's Thumbelina and questions like 'Why would anyone gift away a fairy child to a human?' and 'Why is she so trusting?' and 'What happened to the butterfly when the fairy just upped and left?' and 'Why would the mouse try to match-make inter-species, what's in it for her?' kept popping into my head. So, as always, the what-ifs needed to be hashed out and here you are.

I keep thanking Lana Maklakova for the idea of the book having alternative endings, one for optimists and one for pessimists. This time, again, I re-wrote the pessimist's ending over and over. Originally, the endings were similar in the way that Etta ended up at the Agency no matter what. But then my editor said 'What if she doesn't? Maybe she cannot go there for some reason?' And a new ending was born with a ray of hope in the form of Daisy – sorry, I couldn't keep it completely glum.

Uncharacteristically, I didn't listen to a specific playlist when writing this one. Instead, you will find lots of visual television references, also a source of inspiration.

As for how Etta fared as a Watcher, look out for one of the previous books, Someone To Watch Over Me. So yes, effectively this fourth book is a prequel to my second book. Since my characters sometimes do what they like, I find myself amazed that so many of my books are interlinked and quite a few of them link back to the book about the Agency of Guardian Angels. Like Sally in King of Time, Etta got her own book. Maybe Morgana will, too, some day.

Cinderellas and godmothers (yes, both in the plural) will be the theme of the next book. Cinders: Necessary Evil.

Hugs-a-bunch,
Sky

About the author

Sky Sommers is a pen-name. The author has published academic books under her real name, so it was necessary to distinguish fact from fiction. (Although law books being about dry facts is a matter of opinion.)

Sky has lived in the UK for six years and London is still a constant source of inspiration. She now lives with her family in Tallinn, Estonia, which doesn't feature in her writing, though, sorry to disappoint.

Notes

---

1   For the adventures of Morgana, see Sky Sommers. King of Time, 2017.

2   Belladonna or the deadly nightshade plant has been used since the early part of the 16th century as a cosmetic as well as to promote relaxation. In small dosages belladonna is used in homeopathy to cure nervousness as well as inflammation of different body parts. In very diluted and low dosages (to steer clear of poisoning), belladonna is found to help soothe the mind and also promote sound and undisturbed sleep. However, using too much may give you the Big sleep. The homeopathic remedy belladonna is prepared using the entire belladonna or deadly nightshade plant. After collecting all the parts of the plant, they are crushed and flattened to extract the juice of this herbaceous plant. Subsequently, the juice is mixed with alcohol to produce an extremely diluted preparation. It may be noted that though the belladonna or the deadly nightshade plant is toxic by nature, the final medicine belladonna prepared using the entire plant does not contain even the slightest trace of toxicity and is useful for treating numerous health conditions. - https://www.herbs2000.com/homeopathy/belladonna.htm Tests on stressed mice (pun intended) have indicated that low doses of *Atropa belladonna L.* has a significant neurotropic and protective effect on behavioural and gastric alterations of mice induced by experimental stress. - https://www.ncbi.nlm.nih.gov/pubmed/11274819

3   For the adventures of Loretta and Daisy, see Sky Sommers. Someone To Watch Over Me, 2016.